LEIA STONE

THE LAST DRAGON KING

Trigger Warning

Infant loss/still birth is spoken of but not shown or described in detail. The dragon king has lost children in the past and it affects his character deeply.

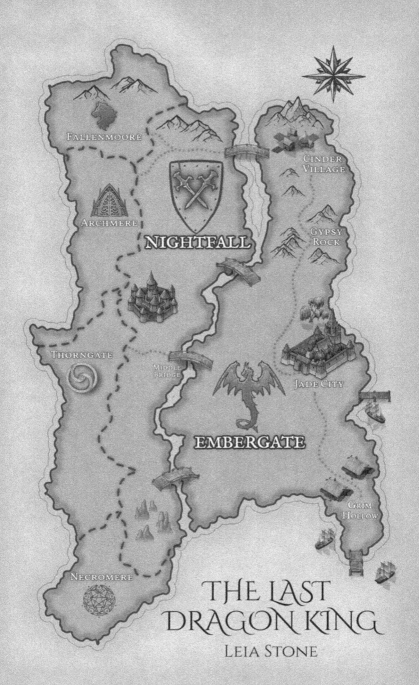

FALLENMOORE

CINDER
VILLAGE

ARCHMERE

NIGHTFALL

GYPSY
ROCK

THORNGATE

MIDDLE
BRIDGE

JADE CITY

EMBERGATE

GRIM
HOLLOW

NECROMERE

THE LAST
DRAGON KING
LEIA STONE

I hauled my kill over my shoulder and grunted under the weight of it. The cougarin had been a full-grown adult male and was my largest kill to date. He would bring enough meat to feed my mother and little sister for at least two moons, as well as give us something to trade at the market. Winter wasn't for a while but I wanted to get new furs for both my mother and Adaline.

Stalking the beast over the last week had proved fruitful and I couldn't help the lopsided grin that drew the corners of my mouth up as I walked into my hometown of Cinder Village.

Being at the base of Cinder Mountain, and the coal mines inside of it, meant that the fine dust from the mountain coated everything in the village, and today was no exception. The rocks that dotted the village road held a thick layer of ash, as did the tips of my hunting boots. I barely noticed anymore; you just got used to it when you lived here. It was in our ears, nose, teeth, and other places not spoken of.

In Jade City, the capital of Embergate, you could spot a Cinder Village resident from a mile away. We puffed dust with each step and we were damn well proud of it. The people of Cinder were a hardworking people. We didn't sit on our butts all day.

"Nice kill, Arwen," Nathanial called from his post at the top of the guard gate entrance to Cinder Village. Nathanial was one of the most handsome guys in Cinder Village. Sandy-blond hair, hazel eyes, and a sharp jaw... just looking up at him now made my stomach warm.

I gave him a goofy grin. "Come for dinner later? Bring your parents."

He nodded, pursing his lips. "Would love that."

We were twenty winters out from the *Great Famine* but my parents remembered such a time and trained us younger ones on how to hunt and grow food, and to skin and prepare a kill. Usually it was the men doing the hunting and the women doing the growing, but with my father dead, I didn't have that luxury. They also taught us to show kindness and give a meal when you had plenty. Times were a boon now, and this cougarin was much more than we needed.

The weight of the animal was starting to cause a sharp pain between my shoulders, its blood dripping down the front of my shirt from the arrow wound in its neck. I couldn't wait to drop this off to my mother and then wash up.

I passed the market stalls, giving nods to the men and women working them, and marveled at the pretty garlands of flowers that had been hung up around the village for May Day. I'd worried that I wasn't going to make it back for the beloved festival of love. I'd made my kill just in time, and if I washed up quickly I might even be able to join the kissing tent.

Pushing my legs faster, I turned the corner to the row my mother's hut was on. We were a simple people who lived a simple life. Thatched huts, fresh river water, potato fields, and coal mining—that was Cinder Village. The ash from the coal mine made the soil fertile and so we were known for our large potatoes and sweet tubers.

I once visited our capital, Jade City, when I was fifteen winters old and my jaw had unhinged the entire three-day trip. It was the most beautiful city in all of Embergate, which is why our king lived there and all of the kings before him. Jade City was full of such opulence and splendor that had I not seen it with my own eyes, I would not have believed it. More jade, gold, and ruby than I'd ever seen in all my life. The roads were all brick, the buildings white stone, the city lit up at night like a jewel. The mead was flowing, the food stalls were stocked, and the streets were *full* of dragon-folk.

I had never been around so many powerful dragon-folk in my entire life, but Jade City had been crawling with them. The dragon-folk were linked to their king, Drae Valdren. He gave them power through himself, and so it made sense they wanted to live near him. Dragon-folk with enough magic had the power to heal, to breathe fire; they had extreme strength. But fully shifting into a dragon's form, that was for the king alone—the most powerful dragon-folk to ever live.

Here in Cinder Village we were a bit of an anomaly. Technically, we were in Embergate territory and ruled by the dragon king, but we were mostly a mixed bunch. Humans, dragon-folk, elves, fae—even a few stray wolven ended up here. Anyone who was of mixed race or of diluted magic was usually outcasted from their territory and wound up here, making a colony of sorts. A mixed breed society. My mom was fully human. Her parents defected from Nightfall City when she was little, and my dad was a mix of human and one-tenth dragon-folk. It wasn't enough to have any cool fire powers, but he was able to lift large rocks in the mines and provide a good life for my mom and I. Until he died when I was nine...

"Bless the Maker, look at that kill!" my mom shrieked from the doorway of our hut, and it pulled me from my thoughts about my father. Every muscle in my body hurt. I was tired, I stunk, and I was covered in blood, but seeing my mom so happy caused me to grin goofily at her.

"We'll need to take out the waistband of my trousers by next week," I joked. My little sister Adaline popped her head out from the doorway as her eyes grew as wide as saucers.

"Cougarin stew for dinner!" she shrieked in joy.

That got a chuckle out of me. The baked potatoes and greens were filling, but nothing like Mama's cougarin stew.

I stepped inside our home, shuffled across the freshly swept floor, and passed the kitchen which led to the back porch. Mother already had the butcher table and knives out. She knew I wouldn't come home empty-handed, and her faith in me made me proud.

After slamming the beast down on the table, I groaned, rolling out my neck.

"You did good, Arwen." My mom smoothed my hair and then wrinkled her nose. "But you smell like death."

Adaline broke out into a full-on belly laugh and I sprang from where I stood and ran after her with my arms out like a bloodsucker from Necromere.

She gave a genuine shriek of terror. Now it was my turn to burst into laughter.

"Alright, don't scare your sister. Go and wash up, it's May Day!" my mother scolded me.

May Day.

I sighed. All the single girls and single boys of age would stand in the village square blindfolded and then start walking towards each other. Whoever you reached first, you kissed.

It was a long-held tradition of Cinder Village, and as terrifying as it sounded it was kind of thrilling as well. Legend said whoever you kissed on May Day would become your spouse. At eighteen winters old, this would be my first May Day. I was eligible last year but had been sicker than a dog from eating some bad berries, so I was unable to attend.

I reached up and touched my lips, wondering if Nathanial would kiss me—you weren't supposed to peek, but some of the boys let their blindfolds slip so that they could gravitate towards the girl they wanted.

I wanted Nathanial.

I slipped into the bedroom I shared with Adaline and grabbed a clean tunic and trousers. My mother had long since given up trying to get me to wear skirts and dresses. Ever since my father died nine winters ago, I'd had to become the hunter of the family, and hunting in a dress was just downright stupid.

Adaline was hiding under her bed furs, probably afraid I'd rub cougarin blood on her. I walked towards her and hovered over her. After a moment, thinking I was gone, she slowly pulled down the covers, but when she saw me she screamed again, yanking the furs back up. I burst out in delighted laughter.

"Arwen!" my mother snapped.

"Fine," I groaned, the laughter dying in my throat.

Sometimes I just wanted to mess around with my little sister, but my position in this family required me to grow up faster than I would have liked had I been given a choice. We had a roof over our heads and food in our bellies, so I knew better than to complain.

"Oh," I called back to my mom as I was walking

out to the community bathhouse. "I invited Nathanial for dinner," I said casually.

A dinner invite on May Day was no small thing.

The corners of my mother's lips quirked up into a conspiratorial grin.

"To be nice! To share the bounty," I told her, heat creeping up to my cheeks. It was customary after a good hunt to invite a guest to the feast. Good luck even. She *knew* that. But it was also encouraged to invite potential suitors over for dinner on May Day so that the families could meet and start getting used to the idea of a potential marriage.

"Of course, dear," she said in a sugary sweet tone, and I scowled at her. I was eighteen winters old. I'd be expected to take a husband soon. Nathanial would be a good choice. He had a prominent job in the village, and he was one of the only boys in town who didn't seem threatened by my hunting trips with the other men in the village. Even when I married off, I'd still have to provide for Adaline and my mother. He understood that.

Brushing my mother's weird smile out of my mind, I headed down the alley between Mr. Korban's apothecary shop and Mrs. Holina's bakery, and stepped into Naomie's bathhouse.

"Oh, child!" Naomie plugged her nose when I

strode inside. "You smell like a dead ratin! You'll need your own soaker tub with extra sandalwood oil."

I grinned.

Naomie was like the village grandmother—with a sharp tongue. She took care of us all and hit us with the truth no matter how much it would hurt. For daily washings I would just use the heated bucket of water in our hut, but for washing after a week of hunting I needed Naomie's soaker tub and soap stone.

I followed her into the women's washroom and past the group soakers, nodding to the women I recognized. Mrs. Beezle and Mrs. Haney were currently enthralled in the town gossip. I caught a snippet of Bardic needing to cut down on his drinking, and Mrs. Namal needing to tend to her husband so his eye didn't wander. The top layer of their bathwater was black from cinder soot.

When Naomie stepped into one of the private soaker rooms, cordoned off by a thatch wall, I set my clean clothes down on the stool beside the small one-person soaker tub. Cinder soot and dirt was okay for a group soaker, but blood and hunting guts were *not* permitted.

Naomie was at least sixty winters old, her fingers gnarled from the winter bone disease. Her silver hair was always tied into a tight bun on top of her head. She spun the tap and the water gushed from the faucet, filling the tub as steam rose up to the ceiling. Naomie was one of the few people with running water in the village. Her shop was directly situated over a natural hot spring. Her great-great grandfather had been a metal worker, so he'd welded the pipes and built everything so that the water would be pulled up from the ground. Her family had owned this bathhouse for as long as anyone could remember.

"I've had to raise my prices," Naomie said, looking at me with a bit of pity. "This war the Nightfall queen has started at the border is affecting my ability to get the soap stones and perfume oils from the elves in Archmere."

I nodded. "How much?"

"Two jade coins or an acceptable barter," she said.

Two jade coins? It used to be one. I'd heard a little about the Nightfall queen causing trouble with shipments coming into Embergate but hadn't thought much about it. That evil woman was always starting wars.

I nodded. "I can give you the jade coins, or I just brought down a full-grown male cougarin. You can see my mom after closing to pick the best cut."

Her eyes lit up. "I'll take the meat instead, thanks

kindly," she said, and I nodded as she slipped out of the room.

Cougarin was gamey but delicious, with very little fat or gristle on it. Elkin was the only more desirable meat around, so I knew I could barter some good stuff with this kill. Maybe I'd get mother a nice new dress for the changing of the seasons festival in fall.

Stripping off my clothes, I let them drop into a dusty blood-crusted pile at my feet and then I stepped into the water.

A groan of pure joy and relief left me, and some of the ladies outside the thin thatch wall snickered. I didn't care. It was too good. As I slid deeper into the water, I felt a few parts of my back sting. At one point in the hunt I'd tumbled and hit my back on a rock. There must be a scratch or two there.

The water continued to rush out of the tap as I daydreamed about having running hot water in our hut. I would take a soak every single night. I'd wash the clothes in hot water, and the dishes, and just for fun I'd stick my face in hot water in the mornings to revive myself.

I sighed in contentment.

"Coming in," Naomie announced before she stepped into the small enclosure.

I didn't bother to cover myself. Naomie had seen

me naked hundreds of times. I'd been coming here since I was a babe with my mother. Besides, she didn't look; she was a professional. She poured a stream of oil into the rushing water and the strong scent of sandalwood hit my nose.

Another sigh.

Cinder Mountain was known for its sandalwood grove trees, so the oil was plentiful here and the scent always reminded me of home.

A soap stone plopped into the water and slid under my back but I ignored it. I'd soap later, I just wanted to soak. Every muscle in my body was screaming out for joy right now.

"Got any cuts?" she asked.

Naomie tended to the men after they came in from a hunt, so she knew what the body sustained after such a trip.

I nodded and sat up, showing her my back.

She whistled low. "The bigger one looks infected. I'll get the neem oil and add it to the bath. The cougarin meat is still a good trade."

Neem was expensive, so it was kind of her not to charge extra or ask for more meat.

She disappeared and shuffled back in with the neem, pouring it into the bathwater as well. She then reached in and grabbed the soap stone as I sat up and hunched forward. She ran it along my back in the parts I couldn't reach and I hissed when she lightly grazed it over the cut. Must have been bigger than I thought. I'd been so excited to kill my first cougarin that I'd lost all sense of pain and just wanted to make it back home.

After getting my back tortured by the old woman, she dropped the soap stone into the tub again and left.

Finally, I can relax.

I leaned back against the angled tub and slid as far down as I could go before drowning. My hair snaked out around me and I was shocked and slightly ashamed to see it looked brown and not blond because it was so dirty. The bathwater had a slight reddish tinge to it from all the blood, so I closed my eyes and just breathed in and out slowly, letting the scent of neem and sandalwood fill my nostrils.

Seven days of stalking the beast and sleeping on rocks and leaves was all worth it now. Gone were the days of hunting small game like rabbits and possums and being ridiculed by the males. I was a respected hunter now—Hades, the men might even let me join the hunters' guild—

"The king's men come this way!" a female voice shouted into the bathhouse and my eyelids snapped open, jarring me from my daydreaming.

The king's men? Were they drafting for the war or

something? Why else would they come here all the way from Jade City? Normally, we brought coal or sandalwood to them to trade; they *never* came to us. We were the dirty forgotten village of Embergate that the king tolerated but never visited or paid any mind to. There were no powerful dragon-folk here for him to draft into his army or be of any use. We were a bunch of mixed breed mutts.

"Listen here!" the same young woman said throughout the bathhouse and I sat up, reaching out to peel the thatch door open and look at her.

Kendal. I should have known. She was the town gossip and lived for any bit of news, especially news from Jade City and anything concerning the dragon king. She liked to think of herself as the town crier. We were friends, but I didn't enjoy her company for too long.

Reaching into her coat, she pulled out some official looking scroll and opened it.

"King Valdren seeks a new wife to give him an heir." She paused for the collective gasp that ripped through the bathhouse, mine included.

He'd only been married to Queen Amelia for three winters and lost four children with her before she finally succumbed to death in childbirth. He had been a young king, married at my age, and was now only

14

twenty-one winters old. Their marriage was the reason I'd traveled to Jade City when I was fifteen. A royal wedding was an exciting affair throughout the realm. Queen Amelia had been gone only a single winter, and without an heir he was vulnerable to the Nightfall queen, who sought to take over this realm and purge it of dragon-folk magic. It was inevitable that he'd seek a new wife, but hearing it official like this was shocking.

Kendal cleared her throat, trying to hide a grin. "He is now opening a full search throughout all of Embergate for a new queen—"

The gasps and shrieks of excitement tore throughout the bathhouse and I couldn't help but snicker at their desperation. The king would never marry a Cinder girl. It was just formality that he announce it here as we were technically a territory of Embergate.

"To bear him an heir," Kendal went on, "he will send sniffers to each town and village and city within Embergate's borders to find *all* eligible women with powerful enough magic to carry his child to term. They must be presented to him by next full moon."

The collective groans of disappointment filled the space. "He's not going to find anyone with powerful magic in Cinder Village!" one of the younger women said, defeated.

"Not one powerful enough to bear a dragon king heir," Naomie agreed.

They were right. Sadly, Queen Amelia died because his magic was too powerful for her to carry his child, and I heard she had been nearly half dragon-folk.

Kendal tossed her hair over her shoulder. "I personally am one-quarter dragon-folk and so—"

The bathhouse erupted into laughter and I couldn't help my own snort.

"Honey, one-quarter?" Naomie shook her head. "To carry a child to term for the dragon king himself, you'd have to be half dragon-folk *and* blessed by the Maker."

Kendal rolled up the parchment hastily and shoved it in her pocket. "We shall let the sniffers decide!" She tore out of the bathhouse, then the gossip started up full-bore.

"Poor young man, losing his wife and four children," someone said.

"Why couldn't she carry an heir? Hades, with my hips I could give him ten children," Bertha Beezle crooned.

I suddenly felt protective over the late queen.

"She didn't *do* anything! The king's magic is too strong for mortal women," I snapped.

Any ounce of humanity the queen carried was torn

in half by the pure-blooded dragon king's magic as she went into labor.

The gossiping died down then and I decided now was a good time to wash my hair and drown out the talking. I'd met her once, Queen Amelia—well, *met* was a lie, but I'd seen her from a distance during my trip to Jade City. The king had already gone inside by the time I'd climbed on top of the flower shop roof and laid eyes on our new queen. She was the most beautiful woman I'd ever seen. Her long hair was inky black and fell in thick curls to her waist. She wore a dress with so much jade on it, it must have weighed as much as a cougarin. It was said that King Valdren and Queen Amelia were chosen as the perfect couple to usher in a new dynasty of magical heirs. How cruel life could be sometimes.

First the king loses his father just after getting married, then his children don't make it to term, and then he loses his wife and stillborn child? It was almost too much loss to bear. So I didn't dwell on it. I genuinely hoped he found a new wife and had a healthy child.

Grabbing the soap stone, I rubbed my body and hair vigorously until my skin was raw and I smelled like an apothecary shop. My hair was now the color of pale corn silk, and other than some bruises and dirt under my nails that would never come clean, I looked decent. Standing, I poured a final clean bucket of water over myself and then heaved out of the bathtub. After brushing my teeth at the small sink Naomie had against the far wall of my private room, I wrapped myself in some linen and pulled the drain plug. Watching the brown and blood-tinged water swirl down the drain, I quickly towel-dried my hair and braided it over one shoulder before slipping into my clean blue cotton tunic and white trousers.

From the commotion outside, I knew that news had traveled fast and the entire village would be buzzing with this gossip for weeks, long after the sniffers came and left.

For the king's men to come to our village on May Day was a big deal.

"Arwen!" My mother's voice came from behind the thatched partition.

I pulled it back and waved her over, but my hand froze midair when I saw the color drained from her face. She rushed forward, grasping me by the upper arms, and leaned in to whisper in my ear.

"You need to leave now. *Run*," she whispered.

I chuckled, wondering what she was playing at, but when she pulled back her face was as serious as I'd ever seen it.

"What's wrong?" I said.

She looked over her shoulder as if saying we couldn't speak here, and I nodded. My body was still with shock; my mom never acted like this. She was calm and very rarely showed fear. Something was up.

Following her out of the bathing tent, I gave Naomie a smile and wave and scurried in the direction of our hut. As we were rounding the corner to our street, I saw the white May Day kissing tent was now set up in the middle of the village. Strands of pink and purple garland hung from the opening. It was picturesque, romantic. The young women of the village were already going inside.

I stopped. "Mother, can this wait? I missed last year and... I was kind of looking forward to..." To my first kiss. I didn't want to say that, but my mother caught on.

She glanced at the kissing tent and surprise flickered over her face. "Right. May Day and you missed last year because of the sickness..."

I nodded, looking eagerly at the tent opening as I saw Nathanial slip inside.

"Mom, please."

My mother walked over to some wildflowers growing in front of Mrs. Patties' house and plucked a purple posey, tucking it into my braid. "Go and have your May Day kiss and then rush right back home. I'll pack your things." She nodded.

I frowned at that. *Pack my things?* I'd just gotten back from a week-long hunt. There was no way I'd be going out again without some proper rest. But she'd consented to the kissing tent so I wasn't going to argue. Scurrying off across the yard, I ran first to Miss Graseen's herbal garden and snatched a sprig of mint. She poked her head out of her kitchen window and grinned.

"Kissing tent?" she asked.

I blushed and shoved the two mint leaves into my mouth, chewing on them vigorously to freshen my breath. Even though I had just brushed my teeth, I wasn't taking any chances with my first kiss. Miss Graseen let us take a sprig here and there, and in turn we all pulled her weeds and mended her fence when predators broke in.

I doubled back, ready to enter the white silk tent, when I craned my neck to the main gate, hearing a commotion.

A large procession of the king's Royal Guard were coming through and headed right this way. I froze, in awe of the horses and their armor. The sunlight glinted across the golden dragon crests on their chests, and I momentarily forgot about the kissing tent. I'd wanted to be in the Royal Guard since I could hold a sword. That of course was not very ladylike and so my mother had discouraged it, but I'd never lost that dream. To my knowledge, there was only one woman in the guard.

Regina Wayfeather.

She was rumored to be the leader of the entire Royal Guard. I wanted to run over and see if she was here and shamefully ask for her to touch my hunting bow for good luck, but I couldn't ignore that my window to get my first kiss was closing. Not to mention that my mother seemed out of sorts so I'd have to run home right after.

As the king's Royal Guard dismounted and started to walk towards the tent, I slipped inside. The bustle of excited chatting reached my ears and my gaze flicked to the other side of the tent, where the young eligible men stood. I locked eyes with Nathanial and he grinned, which caused me to return the smile.

"Arwen!" Kendal called, and I veered to the right, where all of the young women stood in a long row. They were all in their best dresses and had even applied charcoal eyeliner and beetroot lip color, while I stood in linen trousers and a wet braid that Mother had tried to fancy up with a flower.

Now I felt foolish. Who came to the May Day kissing tent in trousers?

A hunter.

When my father died, it was the middle of winter. I'd never forget the pangs of hunger that following year for as long as I lived. The village gave us handouts here and there, but without a hunter in the family to do a monthly trip or work in the mines, we would have surely died. That year, I made my first trap and started bringing back small game.

Ratin was the lowest animal on the totem pole, but it allowed my mother to grieve and not have to rush into a new marriage to try to put food on the table.

I shook my head to clear my thoughts.

Mrs. Brenna, who was hosting the May Day tradition, walked towards the center of the room and cleared her throat. Brenna was human, and one of the village seamstresses. She sewed all of our wedding gowns, so making some lifelong matches today was in her best interest. She always wore beautiful dresses that pushed her giant breasts halfway into her throat and distracted all the men.

"Today may very well be the day you meet your future wife," she told the men, and was met with whoops and cheers. She then turned to the women: "Don't worry, they get better at kissing as time goes on."

The Last Dragon King

We all burst into nervous laughter, and a few of the men groaned at her insult.

I lined myself up directly with Nathanial, then the blindfold came down over my eyes.

"No cheating," Kendal said as she tied it tightly behind my head. I made a slow and deliberate move to raise my blindfold a tiny bit but a hand came down hard, smacking mine.

"This is in the Maker's hands now," Mrs. Brenna scolded me, and my stomach tied into knots.

"Young lovers," Brenna announced, "walk forward and kiss the first person you touch."

The sound of scrambling feet filled my ears as we all stumbled forward, arms out. I wanted to call Nathanial's name, but that would seem desperate. I tried to look down and see if maybe I could recognize his boots, but Kendal had tied this blasted blindfold too tight. Before I knew it, I'd bumped into someone, and his arms came around my waist to steady me.

My heart hammered in my throat. This was it. *This* would be my first kiss.

Please don't be booger-picking Vernon, I prayed to the Maker, and then reached up, trailing my fingers up his chest to find his face. His body froze under my touch and I almost lost my nerve. Was he scared? My fingers slid over the soft fabric until I reached his neck and then paused, afraid to grasp the sides of his face.

His hands were statue-still at my lower back, and I licked my lips to wet them. In the May Day kissing tent, the girls were the ones who made the first move, and you were allowed to back out if you didn't feel ready.

Is this Nathanial?

Did he want to kiss me or run?

Rumor had it that all the guys peeked and Mrs. Brenna let them tie their blindfolds loosely. That if a guy got a girl he didn't want to kiss, then it was a chaste peck, similar to one you would give your mother when young. But if he liked you... rumor also had it that it would make your whole world spin.

I wanted my world to spin.

Because my father died so young, I'd been thrust into the life of hunting and wearing trousers and sharpening my blade. Don't get me wrong: I liked that life, but it made it hard for the other boys to see me as a kissable girl.

I want to be kissed, dammit.

A lump formed in my throat as nervousness built in my stomach. I swallowed it down and leaned forward before I fully lost my nerve. Trailing up his chin with my thumbs, I felt the stubble and sharp jawline of a man that was *definitely* not Nathanial.

I froze, panicked.

Nathanial still had a baby face, no stubble, and his jaw was chiseled but not *that* much. Upon feeling this manly wide jaw and stubble, I wondered if I should go for his cheek. I was so set on kissing Nathanial that confronted with proof this wasn't him, I wanted to back out.

But then his lips were on mine as he made the first move, breaking the cardinal rule of the May Day tent. A small electric spark shocked my skin and I gasped. He did the same—both of us inhaling the other's surprise. Heat traveled down to my core and I leaned forward, deepening the kiss.

His lips were soft and unsure at first, but then they opened and I slid my tongue inside just like Kendal told me to and it collided with his. A small moan escaped him and my world spun as a grin pulled at the corners of my mouth. His hands at my waist stroked a smooth circle on my hips while his tongue did the same in my mouth.

Holy Maker.

This was the best first kiss a girl could hope for. My stomach burned with heat and my heart grew fluttering wings in my chest. The warm pillowy lips on mine made everything in me scream for more.

"Alright, it's getting hot in here!" Brenna announced with a laugh. "Take off those blindfolds and meet your match, my young lovebirds!"

All at once he fell away from me, the lips, the hands, the warmth, the butterflies. It was as if I'd been plunged into a frigid ice bath. I reached up, frantically yanking the blindfold down, and came face to face with the back of the white tent.

He was gone.

An ache formed in my chest. My throat tightened as I cleared it, trying not to show emotion but feeling as if I'd just been left at the altar. You didn't run away from a May Day match unless you thought the kiss was awful and you never wanted to see them again.

I peered to my left and the hole in my chest grew wider. Nathanial was beaming down at a flushed Ruby Ronaldson. Her inky black hair fell in soft waves to her waist, where Nathanial held her hips tightly over her green silk dress. Ruby was a baker. She was feminine and wore dresses and knew how to cook—perfect wife material, and everything I was not.

Tears blurred my vision but I blinked them back. I didn't want to be here anymore, this was stupid.

Turning around, I snuck out of the side opening of the tent and went in search of my mother.

She'd looked so scared earlier, and now I welcomed whatever distraction she was about to throw at me. Anything to forget that world-changing kiss and aching goodbye.

I stepped into our home and the scent of the boiling cougarin stew made my mouth water. My gaze flicked to my traveling pack leaned up against the wall. It had been cleaned and looked fully stocked and ready to go.

"Mom, you're scaring me. Why did you pack my bag? I just got back."

She set my pile of dirty clothes in the washing hamper and then turned to face me with tears in her eyes. "I sent your sister to play with Violet so we have some time to say goodbye privately."

My eyes nearly fell out of my skull. "Goodbye? Mom, I'm not going anywhere. I just got home from a week on the road." Not to mention I just got left in the kissing tent and was now mortified. Whoever my world-tilting kisser was, I wanted to avoid him now at all costs. I wanted to go into my room, cry myself to sleep, and then stay in bed for the next two days.

My mom wrung her hands together, shaking her head, which made her dark brown curls fall away from her face. "I've kept a dark secret from you your entire life," she said and I froze.

I reached out and grasped the edge of the chair, not prepared for those words to ever leave my mother's lips. "What are you talking about?"

My mother stepped closer, picking up my travel bag and handing it to me. "You have to leave before the sniffers find you."

I took the bag but then let it fall to my feet. Reaching out, I grasped my mother's shoulders and looked her right in the eyes. "*What* dark secret?"

It was something you never wanted to hear anyone close to you say. Now I was full-on freaking out. Why did I need to keep the sniffers from finding me? They smelled magic on people and I barely had any. I would be of zero interest to them.

She sighed, and her breath smelled of sage and rosemary, reminding me of my childhood. She loved chewing on the herbs while cooking.

"Your father and I tried for a child for five winters but the healer said there was something wrong with his seed."

Her words cut right through me, causing chills to break out on my arms. What was she saying?

"You *are* my child. My *daughter*," she growled, reaching out to grasp my forearms as if trying to convince me.

That declaration made me sick. Of course I was her daughter. *Why is she telling me I am her daughter?*

"But another woman birthed you," she said, and I dropped my arms, breaking out of her grasp, and collapsed into the chair beneath me. My chest heaved, my breath coming out in ragged gasps.

She fell to her knees in front of me, tears streaming down her face. "I should have told you sooner, but it was never a good time, and I didn't want you to think that you weren't mine."

I sat there in stunned silence for a full minute until she stood again and pulled up the chair before me.

"Who was she? The woman?" I asked, finally able to suck in a full breath and keep my panic at bay.

My mom chewed the inside of her lip. "A traveler passing through. Dressed like a highborn wearing bright colored silk, embroidered with jade. This was when I was still working at the tavern."

I was a *highborn?* Was that what she was telling me? Highborns were at least half dragon-folk, maybe more.

"What happened?" I didn't recognize my own voice. I needed information, and quickly. The hole in my chest was too big now and I needed to fill it with something or I was afraid I would disappear.

My mother swallowed hard. "She came to the tavern alone, heavily pregnant, pale as a ghost and speckled in blood. She looked shaken, like she'd seen a battle. Due to her obvious status, I didn't ask questions. I just showed her to her room."

I waited for her to go on. She glanced at my traveling pack and then at the door and leaned forward. "She went into early labor in the middle of the night. The entire tavern was awoken with her screams. Bardic sent me to tend to her and I did."

Holy Hades!

A woman fleeing a battle was thrust into early labor in Cinder Village? I wondered where she had been traveling to. Cinder Village was at the very tip of Embergate territory, you didn't come here unless you meant to. But highborns didn't come here. Some people had been known to hide here. The ash covered life wasn't desirable, and so not many people came looking. Had she meant to have her baby here? To have me and leave me behind where I wouldn't be found?

My mom's hands shook. "I sent for Elodie. She was the most advanced in laboring at the time, but word came back that she was sick with the black lung and couldn't help."

Elodie died of the black lung the year I was born, then my mother became the village midwife. This must have been the event that started her career! From tavern barmaid to village midwife. I'd always wondered how she made the leap.

"Go on," I urged her.

My mom picked up my pack and walked it over to me, tears streaming freely down her face. "We don't have much time."

I stood, taking the pack and placing it on my back. "I won't leave until I know the whole story. Why do I have to go? Did the highborn die in labor?"

In all my life I'd maybe seen my mother cry twice. Once when my father died and once when she delivered Mrs. Hartley's stillborn. These were far more tears than I'd seen in my eighteen winters.

"It was a full sundown to sun-up labor. In that time we bonded. I told her stories of your father and I to pass the time or distract her. I told her of all the times we tried to get pregnant, where I grew up, anything to keep her from crying out in pain. She told me things too. Scary things."

"What kind of things?" I gripped the straps of the pack tightly.

My mother stepped closer, lowering her voice. "I didn't fully understand what she said. A lot of it sounded like a pain-induced ramble, but one thing I got very clear." She brushed the curls away from her head. "Her entire family was murdered for some type of ongoing feud she had with the dragon king. Her magic was a threat to him she said. She... she said she was a full-blooded dragon-folk."

My eyebrows drew together in confusion. A full-blooded dragon-folk would make her a royal and that wasn't possible. The king didn't have a sister.

My mother went on: "She escaped, but she warned me that if anyone ever detected this magic in her child, that child would be killed."

Full-body chills rushed down every inch of my skin and I froze. "*I'm* that child?"

My mother nodded, reaching out to stroke my cheek as her tears intensified. "She died in labor—too much blood loss. But I saved you and took care of you and loved you and made you *mine*."

A whimper left my throat as I found it hard to contain my own tears.

"I'm so sorry I didn't tell you sooner. It was selfish but I didn't want you to ever think that you weren't wanted or loved." My mom could barely speak.

It was an awful thing not to tell me, but in that moment I forgave her completely. I understood. When was it a good time to tell your child that they were the offspring of a woman whose family was murdered and on the run?

Never.

"I forgive you." I rushed forward and our arms went tightly around each other at the same time.

I noticed now that where I was fair she was dark, and we really looked nothing alike. Not like the other girls and their mothers. Not like her and Adaline.

Wait.

I pulled back and faced her. "How did you have Adaline if there was something wrong with Father's seed? I *saw* you pregnant, I was there at her birth."

I was five when Adaline was born but I remembered it. It was one of my first memories. My mother's screams had scared me.

Shame burned my mother's cheeks and she stared at the floor. "After you came to live with us, your father wanted a second child so badly. He permitted me to... lie... with another man to see if it really was his seed that was broken."

I wasn't prepared for that answer and it must have shown on my face.

"Please do not judge. It is a very much common thing to do, and there was no love or passion between us," she rushed to say.

I wasn't judging, I was just... in *shock*. My father had been a jealous man who once threatened to rip Bardic's balls off if he looked at my mom's cleavage in the tavern. I just didn't see him allowing her to lie with another man.

"He felt guilty he couldn't give me the children we wanted," she said finally. "Tell me you understand?"

I needed a drink. I wasn't normally keen on wine or mead but right now I could drink an entire bottle. I nodded. "I understand." I also wanted to know what man in the village was Adaline's birth father but I didn't dare ask. It wasn't important.

It made me miss my father even more now. He loved my mother so much and wanted another child with her so badly that he let her crawl into another man's bed to have one. It was just another testament to his kindness.

"You must go," my mother urged. "Just say you are going on another hunting trip and return in a week's time. I packed your bag for two weeks just in case."

Another week on the road. The dust, the constant vigilance for looters or stalking animals. Sleeping on a bedroll, bathing in the river, the cold nights... I just got back from doing that. I didn't want to go again, but I knew that I must after what my mother had just told me.

"I'll go," I murmured.

She sighed in relief. "This whole thing will blow over in a week's time. The king doesn't do a census of Cinder Village, so the sniffers won't even know they missed you."

I tightened the straps on my pack and gave her one last hug. "Tell Ada I'll miss her."

My mother nodded and smoothed my hair.

I took one last look at the stew simmering on the stove, a stew that I would never taste, and the skinned cougarin drying out on the back porch, and stepped up to the front door.

"Oh wait!" my mother called. "I almost forgot. The highborn woman also said that she'd put a protective spell on your magic but that it would wear off with time as you come of age. If the sniffers *do* catch you, play dumb. Say you are mostly human with diluted dragon blood."

"Well, I thought that's what I was my entire life," I mumbled. I did have an uncanny sense of balance, I was the fastest runner in my class, and I could track any animal within a mile. I thought it might be the small amount of dragon magic in me from my father.

"Goodbye, Arwen," my mother said, like she would never see me again, and that was unsettling.

"Goodbye, Mother," My voice cracked as I swallowed my emotions.

As I slipped out into the bustling village, I wondered just what in the Hades had become of my life.

There was such an excitement in town from
May Day and the arrival of the Royal
Guard that it was easy to sneak through the
village unnoticed. All of the ladies in town, whether
young or old, dragon-folk or human, it didn't matter,
they all crowded the meeting hall to check in with the
sniffers and ogle the males in the Royal Guard. I'd
never seen a sniffer before but I knew that they were a
magical mix of dragon-folk and fae, with an uncanny
knack for smelling magic. The Royal Guard was likely

present to make sure things remained orderly. As much as I wanted to walk over and inspect their armor and look at the crest up close, I had to leave.

Cinder Village wasn't in any way fortified. We had a front gate, but it was more of a formal entrance than something that would keep an army out. So instead of risking seeing someone at the front, especially Nathanial, and have them ask where I was going, I decided to slip out the side and head for the Great River. The giant body of water divided Embergate from our mortal enemy, Nightfall, and the festering queen who ruled there. She was an elitist that believed humans were blessed by the Maker, and anyone with magic was possessed by darkness. If she had it her way, the entirety of the Avalier realm would be purged of every magical creature and her "pure ones" would rule and multiply.

Shaking off my thoughts of the queen, I made my way to the side gate that was never monitored. Our village walls were thatch; I could cut my way through if need be. These walls were mostly for decoration or to keep muskrats out, not really to deter anyone from coming or going. As I approached the gate, ducking behind a row of huts I was happy to see that it was not only unmonitored, it was open.

Thank the Maker.

Taking one last look over my shoulder, I stepped through the gate and mentally prepared for the week-long journey.

"Where do you think you're going?" a deep male voice called beside me.

I yelped, stumbling backwards, and nearly tripped over a bush as I turned to face the speaker. He wore a deep, black-hooded cloak that covered his face, but I could tell from the brief glimpse at the golden dragon insignia on his chest, and the fine metalwork of his armguards, that he was a member of the Drayken, the elite special operations team within the king's Royal Guard. They were so powerful, I heard that they could light you on fire with a sneeze. Why were the Drayken here? Surely this was a task the regular Royal Guard could handle?

"H-h-hunting," I stuttered.

"Women in Cinder hunt?" he asked, surprise in his tone.

"*This* woman does," I shot back, and put a hand on my hip. How dare he assume I would be relegated to the kitchen or midwifery because of what was between my legs.

"You must not of heard—all women of child-bearing age are to be examined by the king's sniffers," he said. "And you look to be of child-bearing age to me."

That last comment made my cheeks burn. I couldn't see his gaze and yet I could feel his eyes on me. Did I lie and just tell him I was human? I was afraid that the rumors the Drayken guards could smell a lie might be true, but I also needed to get far away from here before the sniffers found me.

"Oh I heard. But I'm a human, so there is no need to—"

The *schling* of his blade made the words die in my throat.

"I smell a lie," he growled.

Hades. It was true!

"*Basically* human," I amended. But even that didn't feel true anymore, not after what my mother had just told me. "Besides, I don't want to get married and have children for a king," I added. I did want marriage and children, but not with the king. I wanted Nathanial. But even as I thought it, my heart pinched to remember the way he gazed at Ruby with his hands tightly secured around her waist.

The Drayken guard barked out in laughter then, and as annoying as it was to be mocked, it was deep and throaty, and almost sounded like it had cobwebs inside of it, like he hadn't laughed in a long time. It made my stomach warm.

"You would turn down the hand of the king?" He sounded shocked and intrigued at the same time.

I shrugged. "I like my life here. What would I do with a thousand jade stones? I can hunt and have all that I need here," I said.

He stepped closer to me and I could feel his gaze on me even though I still had yet to see the color of his eyes or the shape of his nose. The heat of his body was like a radiating furnace, and I swallowed hard as he drew closer.

His head cocked to the side in his hood. "You're telling me that if you were chosen as the next queen of Embergate, and given all the gold and jade and rubies in the realm, you would refuse?"

I was shaken from his question. I wouldn't be chosen as the next queen, but if I were, would I want it? It was a good question to consider. I'd have anything I could ever ask for. I could take hot sandalwood baths daily, I would have an entire staff at my disposal, and my mother and sister would want for nothing. But also after what my mother had just told me and what I knew about the leaders in the village and all the stress they went through, I knew that being queen would be far too great of a responsibility for the simple life I loved.

I shook my head.

"With great duty comes great responsibility," I told him, and his head tipped towards the ground as my words seemingly had an effect on him. "I would not want to trade my simple freedom for one of crushing obligation," I said with finality.

"Crushing." His voice was hollow, void of emotion. "It *can* be crushing at times."

I frowned, about to ask him exactly how high of a position he held in the king's elite Royal Guard, when he put his fingers to his lips and whistled loudly.

I flinched, and within seconds a dark-haired woman ran through the gate with her sword drawn, on alert.

Regina Wayfeather.

She was even more beautiful than I imagined. Wearing black skintight leather battle gear with black chainmail and black shoulder spaulders, her skin was the dark bronze common with the people who hailed from Grim Hollow, our biggest trading port in the realm, and on her cheeks were small patches of black dragon scales denoting her power over the magic. Her long braids hung halfway down her back and were interwoven with golden thread. She was a lethal hunter with a record of leading the king's army in battle many times. She looked about twenty-five winters old, and two long, thin scars ran down the left side of her cheek. But that wasn't what arrested me to the spot. It was her glowing yellow eyes. Her dragon power was engaged; small puffs of smoke leaked from her flaring nostrils.

"She was trying to escape," the hooded male guard said. "Bring her to the sniffers. I can smell her magic from here."

My stomach tightened. *What?* He could? I'd never displayed magic in my entire life. How was he able to tell such a thing? My mother said that my magic had been capped at birth, but now I wondered if it had slowly been opening up.

"Yes, my king," Regina responded with a head bow and I froze, going stock still.

My king?

With his identity ousted, he pulled back the hood and I gazed upon his face.

King Drae Valdren.

I'd seen a painting of him that one time in Jade City but not up close. *Not like this.*

His jaw was stronger and nose sharper up close. His green eyes pierced through me with a quizzical gaze. His long black hair was braided and tied up, as well as shaved on the sides—the typical hairstyle of all the Drayken warriors.

"Your Highness." I bowed my head and did an awkward curtsy at the same time, unsure what the protocol was. I'd just told him things I would *not* have mentioned had I known who he was.

Kill me now and feed me to the cougarins.

I was torn between my mother's warning not to allow the sniffers to access me, and Regina and the king staring at me like they would breathe fire over me if I ran.

"I wasn't running off, I was going on a hunting trip," I told him as I raised my head.

A slight grin graced his lips for a half a second but then it was gone. "Sure you were."

Regina sheathed her sword but her eyes did not cease their glowing. Opening her arm wide, she indicated I walk back into the village.

I nodded, stepping past the both of them, praying to the Maker that I wasn't about to meet my end.

Maybe my mother had been misinformed, maybe the king smelled magic on me because he was the king and he could smell even the smallest amounts but it wouldn't be enough to actually attract the sniffers. And if they did smell some magic on me, so what? Ninety percent of this village had magic—we were magical mutts. None of us were purebred like the king would be looking for.

Right?

Now I wasn't sure. Was the highborn woman who'd birthed me really full-blooded?

I hoped not. For my sake, I hoped she'd snuck into Nightfall City and bedded a human man. I walked back into my village clutching the straps of my pack with white knuckles.

If anyone ever detected this magic in her child, that child would be killed.

My mother's story of the highborn was looping in my mind. Maybe my mother was wrong. Maybe the woman was a raider and had stolen highborn clothing to appear as a noble. Then she'd taken drugs and made the whole story up.

"Why were you sneaking out?" Regina asked me, and I startled a little because I'd forgotten she was behind me.

"I was going hunting," I pressed.

"Sure. The other girls in Grim Hollow ran off *hunting* too," she said with a smile. "You pregnant? Got a boyfriend?"

My cheeks reddened at her insinuation.

"No, I just... I don't want marriage and I like my life here." There was truth in that, and so if she had the same abilities as her king, she would smell it. I did want marriage. Kids too. But not with a stranger and not for duty. I wanted to marry for love.

I peered back to see her smiling. "I don't fancy marriage either," she whispered. "Hard to find a man who will fall for a woman stronger than him."

That caused a grin to grace my lips and I instantly liked her, letting my guard down. I knew I would like her based on the stories and gossip that came through town about her, but especially now that I'd met her.

"Arwen!" My mother's shocked, slightly high-pitched shriek came from the alley.

I spun, my eyes widening. "It turns out that hunting trip will have to wait. I need to be inspected by the sniffers first," I told her.

The alarm on her face was apparent to me but I hoped not Regina. "Oh. Well, let me accompany you, then." She reached out her hand to take my pack and I unloaded it, grateful not to have the weight of it any longer.

My mind spun with what she must be thinking. She'd truly acted in fear for my life just a moment ago. I knew she must be freaking out about this. But maybe it would be okay. The sniffers would do their thing, leave all of the magicless women in Cinder Village behind, and be back on their way.

I wondered what anyone from the village would think about the king hiding just outside these gates. Why didn't he come in? We'd never had a visit from the royal family before. Not as long as I had been alive. The people of Cinder would be honored to meet him and the fact that he hid outside caused anger to unfurl in my gut.

Did he hide because he was too good for the ashes of Cinder Village to grace his royal boots? He wasn't too good to take the monthly truckloads of coal we dug out for Jade City. Not too good to take our women.

Before I knew it, we had reached the great hall. All of the barren and elder women were outside of it, and Regina had to step in front of me and ask them to move in order to make a path.

"They chose Kendal," Naomie told me as I passed.

That surprised me. I'd thought she was too weak in power. She could light candles with her magic but that was about it.

My mother looked to Regina. "Oh, wonderful. We don't even need to continue, then? He's chosen?"

Regina turned and frowned at my mother. "He's chosen many potential candidates across the realm, ma'am." There was suspicion in Regina's gaze. I wanted to tell my mother to cool it. She was going to make things harder for me if Regina thought I was hiding something.

"She's nervous for me to meet the sniffer," I explained to Regina. "We've never met one before and I heard it hurts?"

That wasn't a lie. I *had* heard that the sniffing of magic was uncomfortable, even painful in some cases. I had no idea if it was true or not.

Regina's posture relaxed. "Oh, ma'am, don't worry, your daughter will not be harmed."

"Oh thank goodness," my mother said in a convincing tone, but I saw the pinched expression she wore. With that, we headed into the open double doors of the great hall.

When Regina turned her back to us, I met my mother's gaze and gave her a look that indicated she needed to relax.

She nodded her head, biting at her lip.

"We've got one more!" Regina called over the murmuring voices.

I'd never seen the great hall so packed full of people. The child-bearing women of our village were here with their families, some of them even with their husbands. I didn't think the king's notice included married women. That was awful. What was the chosen queen supposed to do, leave her husband and family to have a second life in Jade City?

Did this man have no morals? He must need an heir badly to be assessing the magic of married women.

The people in the room parted and I made my way up the crowded aisle, feeling like every pair of eyes were on me.

Why did this need to be a public affair? I was nervous enough as it was without the entire town looking at me.

When the throng of people had finally thinned enough to give me a good view of the commotion, I gasped at the sight of the sniffers.

There were two of them, females with bright red hair, and skin so fair I could see the network of blue veins in their cheeks and neck. Twins, I realized, as I scanned their faces. Identical. They each wore a thick black leather eye mask that tied behind their heads and covered their blindness. The tips of their fae ears poked out of their hair, and they cocked their heads to the side in unison as I approached.

Kendal stood proudly behind them as the rest of the girls, rejects I suspected, hugged the walls and watched.

"Bring her to me," one of the twins said, and I gulped. Many, *many*, rumors surrounded the sniffers.

One was that they were born blind, which enhanced their sense of smell. Another was that they weren't blind at all but that their mothers bound their sight with masks to force a magical smell enhancement.

Now that I saw the black leather masks, I wondered if the latter was true and what it would be like not so see anything your entire life by choice.

Regina nudged my back slightly and I steeled myself, looking back at my mother for one last glance.

I expected to see terror, but instead there was determination and the glint of steel in her hand.

Oh Hades.

My gaze narrowed in on the glint of steel in my mother's hand. She had pulled my hunting knife from my pack! My eyes widened, my mouth going slack, but then I quickly fixed my face so that Regina wouldn't see.

What the Maker was Mother intending to do with that? Stab the sniffers? My mom hadn't killed a thing a day in her life, never even swatted a fly. This whole situation had turned her mad.

I stumbled forward, and without seeing me the sniffer reached out and laid a hand on my shoulder.

My heart pounded so hard in my chest I could feel it in my ears.

Another hand landed on my other shoulder, and I looked up to see the second sniffer.

As if they were one being, they both inhaled at the same time, tipping their heads back as if to devour my scent.

I flinched, feeling like my entire soul lay bare in that moment. Something, some magic caressed me then, slithering over my skin and worming into my chest. My breathing became ragged and they both smiled at the same time.

"Sandalwood," the one on the left said.

"Neem," said the one on the right.

"Blood," they both said together.

"And a *whole lot* of magic," the one on the left said with nostrils flared.

Hades.

"Enough to bear the king a child?" Regina's hopeful voice came from behind me, and I steeled myself.

They both shrugged at the same time. "More than this girl." They flicked their head to Kendal and spoke

53

(Leia Stone)

in unison as if sharing one mind. "But not as much as the girl from Grim Hollow."

I sagged in relief. There was a girl in Grim Hollow with more magic than both Kendal and I. *Thank the Maker.*

"Well, bring them both anyway," Regina told them and I went rigid under their grip. "They'll need to be properly tested, and in the end it's the king's decision who he chooses."

Bring them both where?

Kendal and I? *To Jade City?*

Their hands fell away from me and I slunk over to stand with Kendal, wanting to get away from the sniffers' flared nostrils.

My gaze went to my mother, who was watching the sniffers coldly, and I observed her put the hunting knife back into my pack.

Relief rushed through me.

"Would the families of the two chosen girls please come up to the front to speak to me?" Regina called out loudly. "Everyone else may leave."

No one moved. It seemed they didn't want the show to end. "Out!" Regina bellowed, and that got everyone to shake out of their trance. Funnels of people headed for the doors as Kendal's mother and father warily stepped closer to Regina. I watched as my

54

mother shouldered my heavy pack and followed them to stand before the leader of the Royal Guard.

The sniffers started to shuffle out of the room, but halfway through the space they stopped and both turned over their shoulder to look at me. Inhaling again, one of them actually moaned, and then they left.

"Creepy," Kendal whispered, but I found that I wasn't fully in agreement. It *was* creepy, but they also fascinated me. The way they walked, with no canes, it was almost as if they could sense the chairs and people in their way and moved to avoid them. If anything creeped me out, it was their sheer power, which I simultaneously respected.

Regina pulled out a piece of parchment and faced Kendal and I. "Have you both started your monthly bleeding cycles?" she asked flatly.

My eyes widened at the direction of her questioning. She gave me an apologetic look and I nodded. Kendal's cheeks burned as she looked at her father, who cleared his throat, but she nodded as well. Talking about the monthly bleeding in front of men wasn't done in Cinder Village. We kept that private among women only.

Regina seemed to pick up on that and muttered an apology to Kendal.

"Have either of you ever been pregnant before?" she asked us, and we both shook our heads in unison.

I didn't know how they did things in Jade City, but here the young women kept their purity until marriage. Sure, some of the girls bedded the men in secret but it wasn't spoken about or aspired to. If a rumor spread about your purity being taken before marriage, no respectable man would have you.

She checked something off on the parchment and then asked our full names. After writing them down, she faced our parents.

"Kendal and Arwen will be taken by the protection of the Drayken Elite Royal Guard into Jade City to live until the king makes his choice for next wife—" Kendal squealed in excitement and Regina paused. "For each moon that they are away, you will be paid five hundred jade coins."

Kendal's mother and father gasped in shock, but my mother stayed quiet, her eyes narrowing at Regina.

"And what if I don't want to sell my daughter to the king?" my mother asked boldly.

I went rigid. A look of shock crossed Regina's face. "Ma'am, no one said anything about *selling* them. You will be fairly compensated for their temporary absence—"

"I can't eat jade coins. My daughter is a hunter,

and without her we don't have food and neither does a small percentage of this town," my mother said with venom in her voice.

What she said was partly true. I had become a prominent hunter in the village, and what meat we didn't eat, we sold or bartered to others, but after the cougarin I caught today we would have food for at least two moons. The jade coins would be good for other things, and she could barter them for food with the neighboring townspeople of Gypsy Rock if need be.

Regina nodded to my mother. "If you would let me finish what I have to say, you will find that the compensation package also includes meat, dried fruits, yeasted bread, and chocolates, delivered every fortnight."

"Chocolate?" Kendal's mother perked up.

My mother fell silent. There was nothing else left to argue about without looking suspicious.

"Your daughters will be treated as highborns, with a maid staff and private quarters in Jade Castle," Regina went on, and I could see the defeat fall over my mother's face.

"Because we do not wish to bring them away from their culture and the comforts of home, they may each bring one maidservant from their home city if desired," Regina said, and I perked up. I met my mother's gaze and wondered if Adaline was too young to bring. Probably. She still needed to be sung to sleep at night by our mother. My mom shook her head slightly as if reading my mind, and I nodded.

I'd go alone, then. It was better that way. Maidservants weren't a thing in Cinder Village, so I doubted Kendal would bring anyone either.

"In the event of a marriage proposal, a new compensation package will be presented to you at that time. If you agree, please sign here, and know that you are doing the entire kingdom a great service." She pulled two smaller parchments from her satchel.

I expected her to hand them to our parents, but she handed them to us, each with a pen.

Kendal went beet red as she held the pen and I knew why. She had never learned to read. As a seamstress, she really had no need for it. I only learned because I'd started out with an apprenticeship with the town scribe until my father's death, when a year of crop blight on Mother's potatoes forced me into hunting so that we could survive.

I pointed to the part that said *Sign Here* and Kendal took her pen and drew a large X.

I looked at Regina for a split second and found that she watched me curiously.

What happened if I didn't sign? Would it bring shame to Cinder Village? To my family? Would the king march in here himself and throw me over his saddle and take me by force? It didn't feel like I had much of a choice. If I fought this, they might take me anyway but then refuse the offer of jade coins and food, and then where would I be?

I purposely didn't look at my mother. I didn't want to see her urgency for me to refuse.

I scanned the document to find that it said everything Regina had promised and it was signed by the king himself.

Five hundred jade coins.

I quickly did the math. We needed about fifteen jade coins per moon to get by. Five hundred meant that my mother and Adaline would have a full belly in a warm house for the next *three* winters. It meant so many things for our life. And the contract said five hundred jade coins *per* moon cycle. It didn't say only one moon cycle. So I'd go there and I'd watch the king woo this Grim Hollow girl, all the while collecting my jade coins and yeasted breads. Then I'd come back fat and rich.

I grasped the pen and scribbled my name before I could convince myself to back out. My script was awful. I'd never practiced as much as the others in my scribe class, but my name was still legible on the line.

Arwen Novakson.

"Great. We should get going. We'd like to hit Gypsy Rock by nightfall." Regina took the contracts from us and slipped them into her pouch. "Pack whatever you like. I'll have the porter load the wagons."

"It's May Day! Can't we have the dinner feast with them?" my mother asked, the disappointment apparent in her voice.

Regina sighed and faced my mother. "I'm really sorry, ma'am. We've been on the road for an entire moon. Traveled from Grim Hollow all the way up here. This is a matter of the crown, and cannot wait."

With that, she clapped her hands as if to hurry us, and I strode across the room to my mother. When I reached her, she turned around and walked out, giving me her back. A pang of sadness and rejection rushed through me, and I trailed behind her.

"Follow them, Nox," Regina told a fellow Drayken who was standing by the front door.

She didn't trust me and I didn't blame her. I'd tried to avoid this whole thing with a fake hunting trip, and my mother was being cagey and strange.

We didn't speak the entire walk to our hut, and when we reached the door my mother asked Nox to wait outside, which he obliged.

When she finally walked back into my room and

faced me, my gut tightened at the tears that ran down her face.

"I failed to protect you," she said.

"What? No." I rushed forward to console her. "Mother, I'm fine. There is some more powerful girl in Grim Hollow. He'll marry her and forget about me and we'll have five hundred jade coins!"

My mother shook her head. "What if your power grows each day? What if by the time your magic is tested you are more powerful than the Grim Hollow girl?"

"Then I'll run away," I murmured.

My mother looked at me disapprovingly. "He's the dragon king of Embergate. There is nowhere you could go that he could not follow."

Chills ran the length of my spine at her declaration.

My mother stepped forward, placing her hands on my shoulders. "If it looks like your power is discovered, and it's clear that you might have a magic that is greater than even he contains—"

"Mother, that's not possible!" She'd gone mad and was paranoid. Now I was really scared.

She leaned closer to me, her grip on my shoulders tightening. "Listen to me, Arwen. If it *appears* to go that way, that your magic might be a threat to him somehow, then you make him fall in love with you so he won't kill you. Understand?"

Kill me? Kill me because my power would be greater than his? Wasn't that what he wanted? *Maybe not.* Maybe he wanted a woman with just enough power to give him an heir but not too much? Like Regina said, a man doesn't want a woman stronger than him. Maybe that's what had happened to the woman who'd birthed me.

For the first time since this whole thing started, I was genuinely terrified.

"How? How do I make him love me?"

Red colored my mother's cheeks. "Your body can do certain things that a man craves. Make him think of that every time you are in the room, but don't give it to him until you're married."

Now it was my turn for my cheeks to go red. She meant *bed* him.

Kendal had told me *all* about that. She'd learned everything from her aunt who worked in Gypsy Rock, was only two winters older than us and... uninhibited.

"Oh. Okay," I muttered with embarrassment.

Marry him? Was she serious?

"If it comes down to it, you be the strong queen he wants and give him many heirs, but make sure he adores you so that when you're done having children for him he doesn't kill you."

My mother's counsel was harsh. He wouldn't do that, would he? What decent man would?

All I'd heard of King Valdren was of how kind he was to his people, how much he cared for his late wife, Queen Amelia. He saw her through every loss of child —everyone loved him. He was kind... right?

Kind enough to wait outside the gates of Cinder Village? Kind enough to call his guard on me and pull his blade? Kind enough to remarry quickly simply for an heir?

These thoughts scared me, so I shook my head to dislodge them.

Tears welled in my eyes. "Adaline... should I go and say goodbye?"

But my mother shook her head. "She'll be too distraught and make a scene. Leave her a note and send her a gift with the first food shipment."

I nodded, walking to our shared nightstand, and pulled out a torn scrap of paper and a pen. I'd taught Adaline and my mother to read and write during my two-year apprenticeship with the scribe.

Dearest Adaline,

I love you more than all of the jade stone in Jade Mountain. Take care of Mother. I'll send a gift from Jade City.

P.S. Don't be a brat.

Love, Arwen

I hated leaving her like this, especially after our tiff this morning, but Mother was right. She would throw a huge fit and I didn't want to leave the village crying.

"Ma'am…" The guard's voice carried into the house and my mother groaned.

"You come in and take our daughters and give us five minutes to pack them up and see them off!" she yelled back at him. He said nothing in response.

"Mother, be kind," I told her.

I knew she was flustered, but now I worried if she'd made trouble for me in Jade City. If Regina and now Nox thought my mother unkind, they might make life hard for me.

My mother and I grabbed the trunk at the end of my bed which held the winter furs and started to pull them out and put in more practical items. Jade City was near the ocean; it didn't snow there. I started to pack my things and my mother slipped out of the room. "Be right back."

When she returned, she was holding the most magnificent leather armor I'd ever seen.

"Mother!"

She grinned. "Kendal and I have been working on it all year. It was supposed to be for your birthday. These are all of the pelts you've killed. Each one put food on our table."

She laid it on the bed and I sat there, stunned. It was shiny, well-oiled bronze leather that had been stitched together piece by piece. Each piece from a different animal. I recognized the darker muskrat hide. Mother and Kendal had placed it in the center of the corseted chest, and then Kendal had carved swirls and flowers into it, which she was known for. The shoulder spaulders were such a delicate filigree that I couldn't help but reach out and touch it.

"I... can't accept this. It will get stolen or I'll ruin it. It's too nice." It was nicer than the Royal Guard uniforms. More detailed in artwork and embell-ishments.

"Hogwash, you're in the running to be queen. You'll wear it well," my mother said.

I grinned. "You're right. Should I wear it now?"

My mother nodded and I slipped out of my tunic and trousers and she helped me into the skintight hunting suit. There were leather cuffs that buttoned on, and a matching waistbelt with a purse for jade coins. The left armpit pinched a little but I said nothing because Mother was staring at me with tears of happiness in her eyes. Kendal could help me loosen that left seam a little in Jade City.

"It's perfect," I told her and did a spin.

She nodded, holding her throat as she showed more emotion in the last few hours than the entirety of my life.

"I... I know today has been a lot and I hope you still feel... like my daughter," she whimpered.

The fact that she would think anything different tore my heart in two. It was not uncommon when a mother died in labor that an aunt or female friend took the baby in as their own. The child was loved and happy and was none the wiser. That's the same as what had happened here, except this woman had been a stranger and my mother did a kind thing. "I'll *always* feel like your daughter." I could barely speak through my emotions.

"Arwen?" Regina's voice called from the doorway and my mother flinched.

"You can't even stay the night?" she asked me. "You have to run back to Jade City right away?"

I reached out and grasped her hands. "It sounds like they'd been all over the realm and this is their last stop. They must also be eager to get back to their families."

My mother nodded and pulled me in for one last hug. I cherished the moment. This was a genuine hug between me and my mother, who I now knew didn't birth me and yet I loved her no less. After we pulled away, she clasped my trunk and then stepped outside the room.

"Porter!" she called through the house in a snotty Jade City accent that had me snickering.

Seconds later, a man appeared wearing a long traveling cloak and took my trunk on his back like it was made of air.

Magic?

He was short and skinny so it had to be. This display of magic was typical of dragon-folk who lived in Jade City and were very powerful.

I followed my mom to the doorway, where Regina stood beside Nox, the other member of the Royal Guard. A quick glance at their chest plates confirmed my suspicion. Nearly all of the guards here were not just Royal Guardsmen, they were Drayken. The king had brought his most elite team with him to search for a wife.

The question was *why?* His own people wouldn't hurt him. Was the skirmish with the Nightfall queen at the border bigger than I realized?

"I'll see you off here. I don't fancy crying in front of the whole town," my mother said with barely restrained emotion.

I nodded, giving her a last hug, and then with trepidation stepped out the door of my childhood home. Looking over my shoulder, I frowned at the boiling pot of stew.

After a week's worth of hunting, I didn't even get a bowl of Mother's cougarin stew. This Jade City castle chef better be the best damn food artisan in the realm, because I was hungry.

"Nice armor." Regina raised an eyebrow in surprise at my outfit change. We'd just left my street and were stepping over to the horse and carriage that waited in the middle of town.

"Thank you. Kendal and my mother made it," I told her dryly. I liked her, she was my idol, but I didn't like that she was taking me away from everything I knew and loved.

She looked surprised again, and I wondered if she

thought only the palace seamstresses at Jade City were capable of such talent.

"Sorry about my mother. She's... protective," I mentioned to Regina, suddenly a bit embarrassed about how bold my mother had been to her and Nox.

"Good mothers are," she replied, and then had my trunk loaded onto the black carriage that was hitched to two royal horses. There were a dozen horses waiting at the gate, all with Drayken riding on them. The horses were all black with braided tails, and I dreamed of one day riding on one like the Royal Guard did. Maybe I could learn in Jade City, make the most of this time there while the king flitted about trying to make an heir.

Speaking of the king... I scanned the group of guards, my gaze landing on the one with his hood up.

The village people had no idea they were in the midst of royalty.

The main village baker, Mrs. Holina, and Naomie, rushed forward to hand us each a package.

"To remind you of home," Naomie whispered.

Mrs. Holina shoved two steamy hot loaves of rosemary bread at us and my mouth instantly salivated. Even though I knew we'd be back in a moon's time, maybe two, I still felt sad to leave this place... it felt like goodbye.

"Thank you." We hugged them and then stepped into the carriage. I'd only ridden in one once, on my trip to Jade City, but that was more of a covered cart than a regal carriage. This was black lacquered outside with inlays of jade and gold, and the inside was just as nice. Green crushed velvet lined the walls, and the seats were plush and comfortable. There was a small basket of fresh fruit and a canteen of water on each seat. Folded next to all of that was an accordion hand fan made with purple silk to stave off the heat.

"Oh, I could get used to this." Kendal grabbed a passion berry and popped it into her mouth.

I smiled and cradled the package Naomie had given me. It was heavy in my hands and I peeled back the paper, letting a little gasp of surprise escape my throat.

An entire *bottle* of sandalwood oil. That was a very kind and generous gift. Kendal had one too, and was holding hers with unshed tears in her eyes.

"I'm going to miss home," Kendal shared, and I nodded.

"We'll be back soon enough," I said as the cart jerked forward and the horses began our journey.

Kendal frowned. "Hopefully not. Hopefully, the king chooses me and I never come back."

Oh.

I guessed that's what I should be feeling too, but I wasn't. I was hoping he chose the girl from Grim Hollow, or Kendal, so I could just come back here and get on with my life.

We stopped at Gypsy Rock for the night. The day of travel had been long and my butt was numb. It was going to be a three-day journey, and Gypsy Rock was nicer to stay at than the sand dunes, so I wasn't going to complain.

"Ladies, I've booked us a shared room at the tavern," Regina said. "I hope you don't mind, but until we get to Jade City it's not safe for you to sleep without a guard in the room."

Kendal and I nodded. We could sleep in a barn or inside the carriage, and often did when traveling, so it didn't matter to us.

As we stepped up to the tavern doorway, I looked over my shoulder to watch the rest of the Drayken stow their horses in the barn and talk to the stable maid. The king wore his hood high up over his head, obscuring his identity. Kendal had no clue the king rode with us, and I wasn't going to say anything about it. He was keeping his identity secret for a reason, and I didn't want to put him in danger by mentioning it. He might have been a jerk earlier by pulling his blade on me, but I didn't want him dead. If he rode with a hidden identity, it was for a reason.

"Come on. Dinner awaits," Regina said, and I snapped back to attention, giving her an apologetic smile.

We stepped inside the noisy tavern and I was assaulted with the savory smell of stew. My mouth watered and I prayed that we were staying for dinner. I'd hauled that cougarin from the creek on my back, I deserved a meat stew. Kendal and I had grazed on some of the fruits and bread in the carriage, but I was famished from my week on the road and I wanted meat.

The barmaid stepped over to us with a pitcher of ale. "You're back. Will you be havin' the private dining hall again then, love?" she asked Regina, and she simply nodded.

They must have stopped in here on their way into Cinder Village.

All eyes slowly moved in our direction as more of our group filled the space. People quieted and whispers of king's Royal Guard filled the room.

We stepped around the tables, following the stout barmaid back to a private room with swinging saloon doors. There was a large table that could fit at least twenty.

"Mead for the men, water for the ladies," Regina told her, and the barmaid nodded and left.

"I like a good mead every once in a while," I mentioned with a smile. Especially on days like this.

A few of the Royal Guard behind me chuckled and I bristled, not intending for them to hear.

Regina gave me a pointed look. "A potential queen of Embergate does not drink mead from a tavern—I can find you some wine though," she said.

I waved her off, shaking my head. "It's fine." This propriety stuff was lost on me. I'd never get used to hearing "future potential queen." I didn't like drinking much anyway; I didn't want to let my guard down.

The barmaid returned with a tray full of mead and the men cheered, causing her to smile.

When she left, one of the hunters flicked his gaze to the hunting blade at my waist. "Have you used that hunting knife, young one?" he asked as he sat down and grasped the handle of his giant mug. His knuckles were scarred, as was the rest of him. He was at least forty winters old, and his skin looked like tanned leather. He'd spent years out in the sun no doubt.

Young one?

Adaline was a young one, not me. I pulled out my

hunting knife and slammed it onto the table so that it stuck into the dented and chipped wood. There was still some blood crusted on it from my cougarin kill. "Just yesterday in fact." I grinned and he sat up a little straighter.

Another one of the guards slapped him on the back. "Never underestimate a pretty young woman. My ex-wife taught me that."

The whole table burst into laughter and I relaxed a little.

"Alright, you can put your knife away, young one. I respect you," the scarred man said with a grin, and downed his entire mug of mead.

I pulled the knife from the wood and slid it back into my sheath before joining Kendal at the end of the table.

I noticed she was sitting right across from the king, and from the way she was blabbing on she had no idea. He kept his deep hood up, obscuring his face, and listened to her as she jabbered on about the raids we'd had this year and how dreadful it was the king did nothing about them.

I grinned, enjoying this very much as I pulled out the only empty chair left. It was at the head of the table, next to Kendal and the king. I peered at Drae Valdren, or attempted to, as his face was shrouded.

"It's almost like the king doesn't even consider Cinder his lands. He certainly doesn't protect us as he does the other territories," I said, agreeing with Kendal.

The king's entire body stiffened and I had to fight a grin.

"Of course we don't blame *you*. You just do as he says," Kendal told him, and then turned to the guard next to her and asked him about horseback riding.

The king leaned forward on his elbows to get closer to me and I stiffened, swallowing hard to wet my throat.

"The king sent his most elite Royal Guard to look for a wife in Cinder Village. If that doesn't show a love of the people of Cinder, I don't know what does," he declared.

I narrowed my eyes at him and leaned forward as well. "A love of the people of Cinder? How about visiting us every once in a while? The king never comes, and we know it's because the ashes of Cinder are too dirty for his privileged boots."

The table fell silent. I wanted to drown myself in mead. Where was this hostility coming from? He'd lost his wife and child only a winter ago and I was being a total witch. *But it was true.* Cinder was the dirty, poor, least desirable portion of Embergate, and he never came.

"Do you know what is required of the people of Cinder to host the visiting king?" he asked me coldly.

My heart hammered in my chest and I regretted starting this conversation. The other guards were softly talking, but I also knew many were listening on.

I shook my head.

"The streets must be lined with fresh flowers. Fresh breads, fruits, meats, and cheeses must be offered to him and his *entire* Royal Guard. A private bath-house must be emptied and made ready. An inn with an entire floor just for him. The people must greet him by bringing him gifts and lavish him with praise. For the king to visit a poor village like Cinder would be selfish. It would empty their reserves and harden their hearts to him."

I hadn't moved, hadn't breathed while he spoke.

That's why he stayed outside the walls? He didn't want anyone to know that it was him so they wouldn't be obligated by centuries-old rules to welcome him in an extravagant way?

I wanted to die.

"I'm sorry," I mumbled, hanging my head low with shame.

The saloon doors swung open then and the barmaid entered with a huge pot of stew and a pile of bowls.

"Alright, loves, fresh rabbit stew for the road weary." She set the giant pot down and then waved her hand over it. A burst of fire erupted from her palm, heating up the stew, and I watched in fascination. Only a day's journey away from Cinder Village and already I could see the common people here had more magic than we did.

As she started to serve us, I couldn't help but mull over what the king had said. How many people in Cinder thought the king hated our little village, when in reality he'd spared us an inconvenience this entire time?

Still, he could help with the raids.

The stew was wonderful but I couldn't really enjoy it. Not fully. Not while the entire time I could feel the man in the hood's eyes on me with every bite I took. The Drayken drank and ate and talked boisterously, while Kendal and I kept quiet and to ourselves. Regina had to shush them several times when their stories became "unappetizing for a lady's company." In truth, I didn't mind the gory hunting stories or recalling attacks from times past, but Kendal did. She grabbed her stomach and winced as if it made her ill.

"So your father carries dragon magic, Kendal?" the king asked her from behind his hood. She was starting to watch him with a quizzical eye, no doubt wondering why he didn't even take his hood down to eat.

"Yes. He can create a small fireball at will, and works with the Cinder Village Reserve Army to fight the raiders in the springtime," she said proudly. Her soup had gotten cold a moment ago, and she'd used her one trick of being able to conjure flame from her palm to warm it and look cool.

I couldn't even do that.

Her father was arguably the most magically powerful person in our village, aside from Mr. Korban, who was a quarter elf and had some healing abilities. Kendal's father could create and throw fireballs, which had saved us from bad raider attacks in the past—he was also a horrible drunk. No man was of any use passed out on the floor of the tavern, no matter how powerful he was. But I wouldn't say that. This was Kendal's moment to brag about her influential family lineage, and I would allow her to have it.

Meanwhile, I was the magical dud who ate cold stew.

"That's wonderful," the king said, as if pleased that she was powerful enough to possibly give him a child.

He then looked at me. "And which side of the family does your magic come from?"

I paled, every muscle in my body going stiff. I obviously couldn't tell him that the woman who birthed me was a pure-blooded dragon highborn.

"My father," I croaked. "Barely a quarter I'm afraid." I wanted to throw him off my trail, get him more interested in Kendal or this powerful girl from Grim Hollow. I knew he could smell a lie, but to be honest I still hadn't fully processed what my mother had told me, and my father *was* still my father. So it didn't feel like a lie. The longer I was away from my mother, the less scary her story felt, but I still wanted to have my guard up.

I wished I could see the king's face. Was he scowling at me right now? Or merely observing me quizzically?

"The sniffer said she had more power than Kendal," Regina offered slyly, cutting right through my plan of staying under the radar. "She must not know her complete family history."

I glanced at her with annoyance, but she was looking at the king.

Kendal shifted uncomfortably beside me. "I've never been to Jade City. Is it true there is a college there with a focus in clothes-making?"

Saved by Kendal. I owed her one for that.

"There is," the king said coolly, and I felt like he

was still watching me. It was starting to annoy me that I couldn't see his face.

"Aren't you warm with that hood up? Surely you can take it down for dinner?" Kendal said.

Kendal might be simple, but she wasn't stupid. The hood all through dinner was weird and she was starting to direct all of her questions at him, like she knew he was a man of importance.

The men at the table quieted and cast wary glances from her to their king.

"Kendal, he has a horrible facial disfigurement," I said suddenly, and a few men at the table snickered.

"Oh, I'm so sorry," Kendal said, ever the proper lady.

The eyes that I had suspected were glaring at me the entire dinner suddenly turned yellow, and black smoke began to leak from the mouth of the hood.

I froze.

Regina stood so fast her chair skidded backwards. "Alright. Dinner was great. I'm going to get these ladies to bed. Long day of travel in the morning."

Kendal stood as well, alarm registering on her face, and she curtsied to the men. "Thank you for dinner."

I got up last, glaring at the two yellow eyes inside of the hood, which stared right back at me. "Goodnight," I managed to say, and then turned to follow Regina and Kendal out of the dining hall.

I didn't know if I was trying to make the king hate me so that he wouldn't pick me as a wife, or if I truly disliked him. Maybe a little of both.

After settling into our joined room, I cleaned up in the washroom, pleased to find it had hot running water like Naomie's bath-house, and then went right off to sleep. I'd been sleeping on hard dirt or in caves the past week. This was my first real time in a soft bed, so when my head hit the pillow I was out.

Unfortunately, I couldn't stop dreaming about the two yellow eyes glaring at me from within the hood.

Somewhere in the middle of the night, there was a

loud banging at the door. My eyelids flew open as my
heart hammered against the wall of my chest.

"Regina!" a deep male voice barked.

My vision was blurry with sleep, and with only the
moonlight to light up the room, I could barely see as
Regina bolted across the space and tore open the door.

"What is it?" Regina sounded as dazed as I felt.

"Get to the stables." It was Nox. He peered into
the room as I scrambled to sit up. "Nightfall's army was
spotted crossing the Great River. The king awaits your
command." The guard spoke quickly but confidently,
and it was like frigid snow had been poured in my
veins.

The Nightfall army crossed *into* Embergate?

That was... that was an act of war.

I stood, fully alert as all vestiges of sleep left me,
and ran over to Kendal, who was still fast asleep.
"Kendal, wake up." I shook her and she moaned,
peering up at me with bleary eyes.

"What's going on?" Kendal's sleepy voice pierced
the room.

"The Nightfall queen's army is... attacking?" I
wasn't actually sure, but why else would they breach
our lands? "We need to leave with the king, now."

"The king?" she shrieked.

Oh, right, she didn't know. *Oops.*

"Get dressed. Now," Regina ordered.

I slipped into my leather hunting suit and Kendal put on one of her casual day dresses. Within two minutes, we were downstairs and crossing the street, headed for the stables.

The king was there, hood pulled back, pacing the large open barn. When we reached him, Kendal fell into a deep curtsy. "Your Highness."

He nodded at her and gave me a pinched expression before turning to Regina. "Advise me," he commanded her.

Whoa, so Regina really was in charge of his army? That was so incredibly badass, and yet I had no time to dwell on it because my heart was ratcheting up higher each moment.

Regina nodded. "I suspect the Nightfall queen has heard of your search for a new wife. She knows you don't have an heir. She will try to take you out."

Assassination attempt?

Kendal swayed on her feet as if she were about to faint. I positioned myself closer to her just in case.

"I should breathe fire on all of them and burn them to a crisp," he growled.

I smelled smoke. It was probably leaking from his mouth and nose but it was too dark to see.

"My king, you cannot. What the Nightfall army

lacks in magic, they make up for in innovation. They will shoot you out of the sky with their metal projectiles. You know this."

Chills rose up on my arms. I'd heard of the Nightfall queen's inventions but had never seen one. Metal projectiles like arrows? Or something more sinister? A simple arrow couldn't shoot the dragon king out of the sky, so I knew it had to be more.

King Valdren growled, low and haunting, and Regina stepped closer to him. "You know what you have to do."

The flickering torch barely lit up his face and I saw determination in his gaze. "I will *not* leave you and the Drayken to fight my battles."

Regina burst into laughter and the king stiffened. "That is precisely our job," she told him, and then she pointed a finger at his chest. "My *lord*," Regina growled, losing her temper with him, "you tasked me with protecting you and the women on this trip, and in turn I made you swear to *my* plan. Are you a man of your word or not?"

I loved seeing this side of her. She was so strong and fearless. I could only watch in envy.

A grunt of frustration left the king's lips, then his eyes glowed yellow and sought me, piercing into my very soul.

Then he started to disrobe.

What the...?

First his metal shoulder spaulders came off and he handed them to Regina, then his breastplate. I stood in shock and fascination as he took off his black dragon leather top, exposing his abdomen.

I finally found my voice. "What... what are you doing?"

Regina took his offered clothes and looked back at me. "He's flying you and Kendal back to Jade City, where they will raise the alarm of the invasion."

Fly? She said *fly*. He was going to...

When I realized what was happening, my stomach tightened. The dragon king was going to shift into his animal form and fly!

Excitement and terror rushed through me in equal measure.

I followed her gaze just as the king dropped his trousers and Kendal went completely limp beside me, fainting. Rushing forward, I caught her in my arms before she hit the ground.

"My lord, you're going to give these poor young village girls a heart attack," Regina warned as he stood in nothing but his undergarment.

His perfectly tanned body was chiseled perfection. Skin draped over muscle without an ounce of fat. He had scars along his arms, both long slices that looked like they were from swords, and small puckers from arrows. My heart did feel like it was seizing in my chest, but I couldn't look away. I'd never seen a fully naked man before.

At Regina's words, he gave us his back and then the undergarment dropped.

Bless the Maker.

Seeing Drae Valdren's bare butt cheeks sent a wave of heat through my body as my whole chest warmed.

Regina turned to face me and bowed her head lightly. "Please excuse the impropriety. It's an emergency."

I nodded, feeling like my heart was going to jump out of my chest and fall to the floor. I didn't mind it. There was a thrill in seeing the king of Embergate naked, a thrill that I liked.

I was about to ask exactly how we would be flying out of here when the king let out a low groan and I steeled myself. My gaze flicked to his naked form as he fell to the fetal position on the ground.

I watched in wonder as the tan of his skin transformed into shiny black dragon scales. A gasp ripped from my throat as nubs started to protrude from his back, growing like vines on a tree.

"Faster, my king, I fear the Nightfall army is close," Regina told him, pulling out her sword.

Faster? As if he could control such a thing?

I of course knew about his ability to transform into a dragon, the only one of us with dragon magic who could, but seeing it was another wonder altogether.

The black vine-like protrusions on his back grew into leathery wings as dizziness washed over me and I feared I too might faint as Kendal did. His body bulked and he got onto all fours, his hands turning to claws.

"I brought your saddle in case of such an incident." Regina rushed into the stall which held our carriage and retrieved a giant black leather saddle with a basket on top. I was so overwhelmed with witnessing the magical transformation of man to dragon that I'd totally forgotten Kendal in my arms. She roused then, took one look at the dragon now standing in the stable with yellow glowing eyes and smoking nostrils, and went limp again.

Regina looked at Kendal, disappointed. "Weak nerves."

I wanted to stick up for Kendal but she was right. She was squeamish and fainted at the slightest sight of blood.

I marveled at the king's dragon form. Those who lived in Jade City must see him fly past all the time, but way out in Cinder Village we'd only heard of such a display of power. His dragon stood over ten feet tall, a hulking mass of muscle and scales. His tail flicked to the side and my gaze rested on the razor-sharp spikes at the tip.

I watched as Regina, and now two other Royal Guards, strapped a saddle onto the king's back and then urged us forward.

It was a basket saddle with stirrups, and once lowered in I was able to let Kendal rest peacefully inside of the basket at my feet while I sat.

"In case he has to spin in the air," Regina explained, strapping my waist in.

What the Hades did she just say? Fly *upside down*?

She belted Kendal in, who was still unconscious, and then patted the dragon king's shoulder. "Fly fast. Send reinforcements."

He looked at her and nodded and then started to walk out of the barn. I gripped the sides of the basket as I was tossed left and right. A dragon's walk was way different than I expected, and Kendal woke up with the jostling. She stared up at me panicked.

"The king has shifted into a dragon and is flying us to Jade City," I told her quickly so she didn't freak out and faint again.

The poor thing just kept staring at me wide-eyed and nodded, her bottom lip shaking. Kendal had always been a bit fragile, mentally speaking. I believed some things were just too much for her.

'Hold on. I'm taking off.' The king's voice boomed in my mind and my eyes flew open.

'You... you can mindspeak?' I mentally thought at him, unsure if he would respond.

'I am the king of all dragon-folk. What good would I be in my dragon form if I could not communicate with my people?' he responded, and then took flight.

A yelp ripped from both Kendal and me as he kicked off the ground, flapping his outspread wings. They snapped out so fast that a gust of wind surrounded my body, throwing my hair all over the place.

As he pumped higher above Gypsy Rock, I glanced down at Regina and the Royal Guard that had assembled on horseback. I'd never seen Embergate from this vantage point. The sun was just waking, and early shafts of orange glow emanated over the land. Off in the distance, if I squinted, I could see the thatched gates of Cinder Village.

It was incredible.

"I want to go down!" Kendal screamed, the terror evident in her high-pitched tone.

I wanted to go higher, I wanted to sprout wings myself and fly off into a distant land. I wanted more.

"Woooo!" I couldn't help the shriek of joy that left my lungs as the king cut to the left and zoomed off towards Jade City at a blistering pace. I laughed as the cool morning air pressed against my skin and made my long blond hair whip around my face.

It was the most thrilling experience I'd ever had. I was about to scream out in joy again when I spotted the queen's army in the distance and a stone sank in my gut. Hundreds of speckles of metal glinted in the rising sun, a harrowing fate for the day to come.

Kendal whimpered, her face pressed down into the floor of the basket as she curled into a ball at my feet and held on for dear life. I reached down and patted her back, trying to reassure her as my mind chewed on the sight of the queen's army.

How long would it take us to get to Jade City by flight? Would the king be able to rouse an army in time? Surely not if they needed to make it all the way from Jade City to Gypsy Rock on only horseback.

My eyebrows drew together as I noticed a group of large birds coming closer to us. They were flying above the army, but what concerned me was that the birds' wings glinted in the sunlight much like the men below.

Metal?

The king veered left towards Jade City and I craned my neck to follow the birds.

Something isn't right.

As they neared, I realized how large they were.

'Your Highness...' I turned forward again, trying to mentally communicate with him, unsure how to initiate the process, but merely thought something and then pushed it at him.

'What is it?' he asked, flying us faster and harder than before.

I peered behind us again, not sure that my suspicion was correct. *'You see those half dozen birds behind us?'* I asked him.

He craned his large dragon head quickly over one shoulder and then nodded before facing forward again.

'Yes.' He sounded distracted, as if my chatter was taking his concentration.

I pulled my hunting knife from the sheath at my thigh, hoping I wouldn't spook Kendal, whose face was still buried in her hands at my feet. *'They aren't birds.'* I tried to sound calm, but even in my own head I could hear the terror in my mental voice.

His head whipped back again. His nostrils started to smoke as he squinted, his eyes taking in the human arms and legs dangling from the "birds."

'Another one of the Nightfall queen's inventions. A

flying contraption for a human?' He sounded bewildered.

My heart hammered in my chest as I peered behind me once more. The men were gaining on us, and they indeed had metal wings attached to their backs with leather straps, but it left their arms and legs free to dangle, and right now, in each man's right hand was a sleek metal sword.

'They carry swords!' I advised the king, and looked closer at one of the other bird men.

'Hades!' the king cursed, pushing even faster as his wings cut through the air with ease. *'I hate to ask this of a lady but... can you fight? You said you hunted, right?'*

A lady? I wasn't a lady. Not really. Not delicate and easily spooked like Kendal was.

'Yes,' I growled. *'My knife is already out.'*

'Look down at your feet. There are two stirrups. Slip your feet into those and unbuckle your waistbelt so that you can stand up.'

Stand up without a waistbelt? Was he insane? My hands shook with nerves, just like they did before a kill, and I wished I had my bow. It was back in the trunk on the carriage at Gypsy Rock.

"Arwen, what's happening?" Kendal whimpered. She peered behind us and then let out a shriek of terror.

"Just lie down and cover your head," I ordered her as I slipped my boot into the tight straps sewn into the harness, spreading my legs wide so that Kendal was between them. There was a ratchet type of strap that I used to tighten it until my foot felt positively squished. Better to be too tight than too loose. I unbuckled my waistbelt and then tried to stand.

It took me two tries, but I finally did it, unprepared for the wind trying to knock me back again.

'I'm standing,' I told the king.

'Good. Now crouch down and grab my sword from the saddlebag to your right.'

His sword? The dragon king wanted me to take *his* sword?

'Umm, I'm not sure—'

'That's an order. Take my sword now!' he barked into my head and I jumped, quickly crouching to flip open the clasp that held the flap of the saddlebag shut. When I reached in and came out with the sword, I could barely heft it with one hand. I had to re-sheath my own knife so I could hold the king's blade with two hands. When I held it more confidently, I stared in awe at its beauty. It was covered with more rubies and jade-stones than I could ever imagine would fit in the hilt of a sword.

'Got it.'

'*Good. Now stab anything that tries to drop on my back. I'll take care of everything else.*'

His words didn't feel real. Was he serious? Prepare to... *stab* a man? I mean, I had pulled out my blade for self-defense, but now that I was confronted with the idea of killing a man I felt sick. Elkin, rabbitin, cougarin, ratin, I'd kill any animal that walked, but a man? I'd never killed a man before. I'd never killed anything that wasn't going to feed my family.

The king started to turn, veering to the right, and I realized he was going to attack them head on.

'*Your Highness, I've never killed a man. Only animals. Only for food.*' My chest heaved as I fought for breath.

'*Then pretend they're animals. It feels the same,*' came his reply.

Before I could dwell on it any longer, the fight was upon us.

7

The king flew right at the bird men from Nightfall and I steeled myself. There were six of them, all fanned out in a V formation of varying heights. Just as I was worrying how we would survive these odds, a stream of dragon fire flew from the king's mouth in a blaze of glory, drenching two of the men completely. The heat from the fire warmed my face but did not hurt me.

I flinched as their screams of agony caused bile to creep up my throat. The two men tumbled in the air, and started to spin in an effort to put out the flames. Within seconds they dropped like stones towards the ground, their winged contraptions no longer able to hold them.

I couldn't dwell on the horror of it too long, because one of the flying men who'd been higher above was now dropping right over us.

I realized now that his sword was so long it would have gored me before I'd have been able to even scratch him with my small hunting blade. I was lucky the king had offered his, but I was also about to kill a man, or severely injure him. Or die myself...

He's an animal, he's an animal... I told myself as he inched closer.

The man wore a menacing snarl, and as he neared I noticed the Nightfall crest upon his breastplate. He was human. Someone we were taught was a poor defenseless soul when matched with a magic wielder. But he didn't look so helpless to me now. No one from the Nightfall army was, human or not. For one thing, he was *flying*, and looked like he wanted to take off my head.

His wings retracted suddenly and then he dropped down like a stone.

I was used to sudden movements—the cougarins that prowled the backside of Cinder Mountain were fast—but I was faster. With a battle cry, I lunged upward to meet him, ramming the sword right into his gut as I simultaneously ducked out of the way of his sword. It cut through him like butter, but then the weight of his body knocked me back. I fell hard against the saddle and the cut on my back reminded me it was there with a fresh wave of pain. The man groaned as my blade went deeper into him, then Kendal started screaming bloody murder. She must have looked up. With a burst of adrenaline, I pushed off of the basket, ignoring the fiery pain on my back. Keeping my hands firmly on the hilt of the sword, I used the momentum to toss him over the side, clutching the sword so that I didn't lose it.

His body slid from the blade with ease and down towards the earth. I tried to catch my breath.

'Are you okay?' The king's voice came to me just as he released another stream of fire at two more advancing bird men.

'Fine,' I told him, looking at the blood-soaked blade and the splatters it had left on my new hunting outfit.

I killed a man. I killed a human.

My beating heart and the rushing wind were the only sounds I could sense for a few moments. I found myself offering up a prayer of forgiveness to the Maker. I didn't think protecting my life was wrong, but at the same time I didn't relish what I'd just done.

The prayer settled my nerves and I looked up to see that there was only one man left. A very smart man who was now retreating.

Sitting back on my butt, I let the sword rest across my lap and stared in shock at my hands.

Kendal chose this moment to lift her head. She caught an eyeful of all the blood and let loose with another blood-curdling shriek before fainting.

'What's wrong?' the king demanded, his flight movements jerky as if evading attack.

'Nothing, Kendal just saw all the blood. She's easily frightened,' I muttered, and his body relaxed beneath us. His flying evened out, and once again we were heading for Jade City.

I stared at the dragon king's neck, the shiny black scales and the way they reflected the morning sun. They almost looked metallic, which had me transfixed. I reached out timidly, unsure if I was allowed to, and stroked the skin. His body shuddered beneath my touch, and I snapped my hand back, eyes wide.

Oh Maker.

Was that... was that totally inappropriate? Now I felt stupid and I prayed he'd think it was Kendal, although that was a stupid thought; she was still unconscious in a ball at my feet. An awkward silence stretched for too many minutes and I wondered if I should apologize.

I didn't stroke the king like he was a horse! What in the Hades was I thinking?

When Jade City rose up in the distance, in my head I started gathering the words for an apology. We'd gotten here much faster than I thought we would, flying over hundreds of small stone cottages in the outer city. The solid wall of jade stone greeted us as we flew right over it.

Guards in the towers saw us approaching and blew a long deep horn, signaling our arrival.

King Valdren dipped lower, bringing the rooftops closer. I held my breath as I took in the view of this magnificent city. It was absolutely breathtaking. Children ran through the cobbled streets with flowers, pointing up at the sky. "The king! The king!"

Shopkeepers poked their heads out, and I tried to eye some of the crafts at the market, but we flew by too fast. Jade City had the most beautiful jewelry in all the realm. They were famous for their dragon fire-glazed glass beads. Even with the early hour, the city was bustling with activity, and as much as I wanted to sightsee, there was an urgent matter at hand. I was covered in a dead man's blood, with Kendal now cognizant and quivering at my feet.

We neared the giant Jade Castle, appearing to glow a mint green from the sun's rays. It was truly a sight to behold. Solid jade, five stories high, and wider than nearly all of Cinder Village. It was fireproof, arrow-proof, and just about everything else—the safest place in the kingdom. The king flew around the castle and to the back, near what appeared to be a training ground. There were stables and wide-open fields, and men running around putting on armor and swords. The call from the gate must have been a war call. Or maybe the king mentally called them. I did not know the range of his abilities.

He lowered us onto the grass, landing softly. A guard rushed forward, eyes wide as he took in my appearance. I was still clutching the king's sword with white knuckles and was covered in dry, sticky blood.

"My lady! Are you hurt?"

I shook my head. "Help her first." I pointed to Kendal, who popped her head up and looked around the courtyard at the men preparing for war. Her eyes grew larger than a barn owl's, and her bottom lip shook.

"Let me help you down, miss." The guard reached for her and she accepted his outstretched hand.

As he was helping her down, a short, sturdy

woman with a sharp chin and brown hair that was pulled into a tight bun rushed forward. "Oh, my dear!" she cooed over Kendal.

I leapt out of the saddle like I was jumping off of a tall rock and stood before the king. He immediately started his transition back to human. His men took the saddle off of him and I gave him my back, unsure I could withstand seeing him fully naked from the front. I might faint like Kendal if that were the case. He stepped out from behind me wearing nothing but a baggy pair of trousers and looked down on me with an unreadable expression.

"Are you okay?" His question was full of compassion and concern, and I wasn't prepared for it. I also wasn't prepared to see the definition in his abs up close.

My heart hammered against my chest as I remembered sticking the human Nightfall warrior in the gut. I nodded, and then reached down into the grass, wiping his blade clean.

"Thanks for letting me borrow that," I told him, deciding that an apology for stroking his skin now would be way too weird. Best we both forget it happened.

He cocked his head to the side, his green eyes flashing yellow as he appraised me. His gaze roamed over my leather hunting suit and the blood that covered it. "If I don't make you my wife, I might have to put you in my army." His tone was joking, but I couldn't help the lopsided grin that graced my face.

Could I join the Royal Army? Become a Drayken? The thought opened up something inside of me that I never had before.

A dream. A possibility. *A future with importance.*

Before I could respond, the woman with the tight bun pulled gently on my arm.

"Come on, dears. The battlefield is no place for a lady." The stout woman shooed me forward and I reluctantly followed after her, unable to get the king's words out of my mind.

Was he serious about me joining his army? Because I would be so down for that.

"I'm Annabeth, the head housemaid here at Jade Castle. You must be the prospective wives from Cinder Village?" she asked Kendal and I as we walked away from the men running around with weapons and mounting horses. I wanted to turn back, to go out into battle with them at Gypsy Rock, but I knew it wouldn't be allowed.

I wasn't sure I would ever get used to the term "prospective wife."

"I'm Kendal."

"I'm Arwen," I said as Annabeth opened a door

that led us into an extravagant hallway. The walls, the floors, all of it was solid jade. I'd never seen this much wealth in my entire life and it took me back a bit. So much so that I hadn't realized I'd stopped walking.

"You get used to it, dear. The lavatories are solid gold too," Annabeth commented.

I laughed. She was funny.

She gave me a serious look. "I'm not kidding."

Oh. I shifted uncomfortably and her eyes roamed over me closely for the first time. "You need a bath before you meet the others."

"The others?"

She nodded. "The other prospective wives."

Oh, how many were there? The Grim Hollow girl and probably one or two from right here in Jade City... were there more from the villages near the Great River?

"A bath would be lovely," I murmured, and she motioned that we follow her down another hallway. I was already lost. When we turned down yet another corridor I saw that there were over a dozen doors, each one with a maid standing in front of it.

Holy Hades.

They had maids just waiting for their guests? He must entertain a lot.

Annabeth walked me right up to the last door and

smiled at a young girl with black curly hair who tried and failed not to look shocked at my bloody appearance. She seemed a few winters older than me, maybe twenty winters old.

"There was a mishap, and Arwen will need a bath before lunch," Annabeth advised her.

The young curly-haired girl cleared her throat and curtsied. "Yes, ma'am."

She opened the door and I stepped inside as Annabeth walked Kendal to the room next door, introducing her to her maid.

Kendal gave me a small wave, letting me know she was okay, and I closed the door to my new room and spun around.

"Holy Hades fire," I gasped, and my new maid stiffened. "Oh, that wasn't very ladylike, huh? I need to work on that stuff I guess," I told her. Unless I was going to join the king's army. In that case, I could curse all I wanted.

She bowed deeply to me. "I'm Narine. I am here to help you in any way possible."

I gave her a nervous wave. "I'm Arwen." I bowed back and she went rigid, eyes wide. I winced. "I'm not supposed to bow to you, am I?"

Her façade dropped and she burst into laughter,

which I appreciated. I couldn't live with an emotionally dead person hanging around all the time.

"No," she said, and then cut off her laughter quickly. "I'm sorry for laughing, my lady, I—"

"Oh, please be normal with me, at ease or whatever. I'm not a lady, I'm a hunter from Cinder Village." I showed her my blood and dirt crusted nails and she winced.

"A hunter? Let's get you cleaned up. You'll have to become a lady if you want to marry the king."

I shrugged. "What if I don't want to marry the king?"

Her eyebrow raised but she said nothing, slipping out of the room, giving me time to fully take in the luxurious space.

The carpet was a plush high pile in a deep purple. The couch was a shiny golden fabric that probably had actual gold in it, and the little kitchen area was so clean I was afraid to cook anything in it. There was a sitting room, a bedroom, a guestroom, and *two* washrooms!

It was official. These living quarters were bigger than my hut back at Cinder Village, and *much* nicer too.

"Lady Arwen, your bath is ready." Narine's voice spooked me as I was staring out the window at the lush green rolling hills, where the army was currently drawing together on horseback. There were hundreds of them.

"I wonder if we will go to war with Nightfall now," I mused aloud.

Narine clicked her tongue. "That's for the men to figure out. You need to wash and focus on the competition."

I snorted. "Competition? Is that what they are calling this? Half a dozen women competing for the king's hand in marriage when all he really wants is our magical womb?"

She looked stricken and I instantly felt bad for speaking so brashly. She clearly wasn't used to it.

"I'm sorry. I like to speak my mind," I admitted.

She glared at me and I was a little taken aback by the anger on her face. Without another word, she turned on her heel and I followed her down the hall and into the washroom.

Okay, speak less and stop pissing off the maid, I told myself. I talked a lot when I got nervous. It was a bad trait.

"Oh my Maker!" I squealed when we stepped into the large space. Floor-to-ceiling white jade stone encompassed the room, with a giant copper soaker tub in the middle. Hot curls of steam rose to the ceiling, and a lemon-fresh scent reached my nose. The wallpaper was a gold and purple floral pattern with jade stone border. It was the most beautiful bathhouse I'd ever seen.

"I could get used to this," I told Narine, and started to undress.

"Well, don't, if you don't take this competition seriously," she snapped under her breath.

I'd clearly upset her with my harsh words before. I tried to patch up what damage I'd already done. "The king is a fine man that most women would be blessed to marry."

Again that glare, one that made me no longer want her in my presence. This was not going well. "I can bathe alone," I murmured, and with a curt nod she left the room, shutting the door a little more forcefully than was appropriate.

Holy Hades, this woman was a nightmare! Would it be mean of me to request a new maid from Annabeth? I should be lucky they'd given me a maid at all, but who wanted to be around someone who glared and slammed doors all day? I mean, I had said that I didn't want to marry the king, but was that so bad? Would she marry him if he ripped her from her village and threw her with a bunch of other women in a competition? It was barbaric and wrong. I would marry for love. End of story.

After stripping naked, I dunked into the bath, letting a sigh escape me at the comfort of the warm clean water. I was still angry at Narine, but I wasn't going to let it ruin the bath. That was three hot baths in a row. I should probably ask for a warm bucket of water next time so I didn't get used to such luxuries.

I scrubbed quickly, making sure to get the healing wound at my back, which I could now barely feel. I wanted to hurry, not wanting to soak in the man's blood that I'd killed. When I was finished, I got out and donned the clean blue cotton dress that was folded on the chair and the golden tinted leather sandals that were a half size too big. I looked like I was going for a stroll in a garden. How a proper lady should dress, I supposed.

There was a hairbrush, scented perfume, and makeup on the counter that I wanted nothing to do with. I wouldn't know how to put on makeup. My mother never bought it or wore it, but I did brush my long hair; otherwise it would knot up. I'd had a moment to think now about how ungrateful I must have seemed to Narine about not wanting to marry the king. In her mind, even being considered would be a great honor, and I needed to be more grateful. He was in fact paying five hundred jade coins just to have me here for a moon's time. I decided to go in search of

Narine to apologize and possibly explain my side of things.

It was not easy to be ripped from your home into a new land with an expectation that you might marry a stranger and carry his children—even if that stranger was your king. Not to mention that my mother had warned me he might kill me if he detected my magic which had yet to present itself. I had good reason for saying what I said, but she didn't know that.

I stepped out of the washroom and through a hallway before I came out into the living room. I was about to open my mouth and call out Narine's name when I heard her voice coming from the front entryway.

"My girl won't stop crying, I don't know what to do," an unfamiliar voice said.

"My girl doesn't even want to be here or get married. So I can kiss my prize money goodbye," Narine called back to her.

Prize money?

"Oh, Narine, I'm so sorry. I know how much you needed that money to pay for your little sister's wedding."

Narine growled, "Doesn't matter anyway. No matter how well we do their hair and makeup, and teach them to be proper, the king will pick the most powerful one anyway."

"Annabeth gave us both Cinder girls. She must hate us."

Narine snickered. I'd heard enough.

I cleared my throat loudly and Narine jumped three feet into the air, slamming the front door shut and facing me with her head hung low in shame.

"My lady! There's no excuse for what you heard. I'm so sorry and—"

I waved her off. "What prize money? Is that why you were so upset with me? You get some prize money if the king picks me?"

She swallowed hard, her brown eyes meeting mine, and nodded. "As an encouragement for the maids to do our best in preparing you to meet the king and get through the competition, Annabeth has promised the winning maid one hundred jade coins prize money."

I nodded. That made sense why she'd suddenly gotten so pissy when I'd said I didn't even want to get married.

"And you need the money to marry off your sister?" I asked.

I knew weddings were different here in Jade City. A much bigger, more elaborate affair.

She nodded, chewing her lip. "My mom passed in

113

childbirth. Dad died two winters back serving in the king's army. I raise my sister alone, so it falls to me to pay for her wedding."

Well, Hades, if that wasn't going to make me feel bad, nothing would. I could relate. I took care of my family too. My mom's payments as a midwife were sporadic. There just weren't babies' born routinely enough in Cinder Village.

I frowned. "I'm sorry. I can see now how it would have upset you to meet me, and the first thing out of my mouth is that I hope I do not win the king's heart."

She shook her head. "Still, there is no excuse for what you overheard me say. If Annabeth knew—"

I scoffed. "I'm no snitch! Your secret is safe with me. We all need to vent to someone. I'm glad you have a friend."

Her head snapped up as shock ran across her features. "You're not mad? You won't tell?"

I shrugged. "I mean, I don't love that you made girls from Cinder sound like bottom feeders, but nah, I'm not mad." I collapsed onto the couch and kicked my feet up onto the little table in front of it.

She sighed in relief. "Thank you, my lady. I'll be more respectful from now on, I promise. And nothing against Cinder Village. I just assumed they wouldn't have the most magically powerful women there since it's mostly full of humans and half-breeds."

Cinder was known for that, so I couldn't be mad at that assumption.

I rubbed my chin. "I'm assuming there will be fancy balls and dinners I'll go to?"

Her eyes lit up. "Oh, yes, miss. Annabeth has coordinated multiple events to help the king get to know all of the ladies present."

"And I assume I will be given a fancy dress for such occasions?" I motioned to the day dress I wore now. Even though it was only cotton, it was dyed an expensive shade of blue; ruffles at the neckline and hem were fancy detailing we didn't do in everyday dresses in Cinder Village.

She bobbed her head eagerly. "Oh yes, I'm supposed to take you to the dressmaker now so that she can get your measurements."

I grinned and stood. "Then I'll tell you what. Each and every dress I get or any other gift, I will wear once and then give to you so that you can sell it to help pay for your sister's wedding."

Her mouth popped open and then shut and then opened again. "That's surely not allowed."

"Why not? Are they not gifts to me to do as I please?" I asked.

Excitement lit up her eyes. "You would do that? After what I said about you?"

"I would. Because I too have a little sister, and I know what it's like to want things I can't afford," I told her.

A lopsided grin graced her mouth. "I guess I'm lucky I got a Cinder girl, then."

"I guess you are." I chuckled.

I spent over an hour with the seamstress begging that as well as dresses she also make me three pairs of trousers and some short tunics. She said no the first three times, saying that trousers and tunics were not for women. I then asked her if Regina was a woman, and who had made her trousers and tunics. She'd simply sighed and said she would make them. Then I further pleaded that she try to get the blood-stains out of my leather hunting suit that my mom gave me. Once she agreed to everything, I thanked her profusely and then followed Narine to the luncheon.

"The king is off dealing with matters of the realm, so he won't be joining you for lunch," Narine told me.

Matters of the realm. AKA the Nightfall queen attack on Gypsy Rock I was dying to know about. I could care less about having lunch with the king, I wanted to know how the attack was going.

"Do we have word from Gypsy Rock? How is the fighting going?" I asked her.

She raised one eyebrow at me. "How do you know about that?"

I waved her off. "I was there. I rode here on the dragon king's back! Where do you think I got all that blood from?"

She nodded. "I heard. I cannot say too much, but I do have a source that said a messenger just arrived a few minutes ago."

I stopped in the hallway. "And...?"

She looked at me with a bewildered expression. "I don't know, I wasn't there, and they are private messages meant only for the king and his advisors."

I folded my arms over my chest and scowled.

Narine gestured to a large set of double doors. "This lunch will be a good time for me to assess your table manners."

I couldn't help the peal of laughter that escaped me. "Narine, please don't bother. My mother fed us meat on the bone in front of the fireplace since I was a wee babe. I'm not going to be impressing anyone with my table manners."

She sighed, and I saw the moment she gave up on me. The light died in her eyes as she gave up hope that I would be some refined Jade City queen.

I stopped in the hallway and leaned closer to her, lowering my voice. "Listen, if you *really* want to try to win this thing, I could ask for another maid. There's a girl from Grim Hollow that I overheard the king's lead guard saying was very powerful. Maybe you could be with her?"

She gave me a polite smile. "We can't switch."

I figured as much. "Well, then we'll just do the dress resell thing?"

Another polite smile. "Yes, lady. Thank you. It's a kindness I won't forget."

I felt better about patching things up with her and having an ally, but still felt a little guilty I wasn't trying to marry the king and win her those one hundred jade coins.

She opened the doors and I stepped inside the room. I was instantly assaulted with the sight of over a hundred women in colored dresses and gold leather sandals.

Holy Hades.

I looked at Narine. "Are we in the right place?" I asked, although in my gut I knew that we were. I knew in that moment that the king had summoned every female of child-bearing age with an ounce of magic in them.

"We are."She nodded.

I felt simultaneously dirty and relieved. Dirty that we were all dressed the same, given the same dress and sandals like brands on cattle, but relieved that there were so many women there was no way the king would ever pick me as his wife in a sea full of other women. I just wasn't that special, and my magic still hadn't even shown itself. With luck, I'd be home by the next full moon and King Valdren would have his wife with her magical baby-making womb.

"Food!" I ran over to the table Kendal was sitting at and took a seat next to her. She was chatting with some of the other girls, and in the middle of the table was a smorgasbord of various cuisine. Meats, cheeses, small fancy breads, and tiny little pies littered the table. I grabbed two of everything and piled my plate high, digging in.

Narine pulled up a chair next to me and watched me.

I moaned, dipping one of the little meat pies into some kind of spicy cheese sauce that I'd never had before. "Holy Hades," I moaned again.

Narine smacked my shoulder lightly. "No moaning, and no cursing at the dinner table," she chided.

Kendal snickered, as well as two of the other girls. "Oh, you won't be teaching this one manners," Kendal jibed, but smiled so that I knew it was playful. After seeing her faint so many times and hearing from her maid that she'd been crying, my heart felt for her. Back in Cinder I didn't hang out with her often. I wasn't a fan of gossip and the latest fashion, so we just didn't have a lot in common, but here... here we were Cinder girls and we needed to stick together.

I nodded, looking to Narine. "You might as well spend my mealtimes doing something you love. There's no saving me." I shoved a gigantic bread roll into my mouth to make a point and Narine visibly shrunk, wincing in slight disgust.

"Alright, well, if you're sure."

"I'm shlure." My voice was muffled through the bread roll. Narine reached up to rub her temples.

Once she left, I swallowed the roll and smiled at my

triumph. I wasn't technically that bad at the dinner table, but I wasn't about to get some propriety lessons like a Jade City girl. I wanted to eat in peace and talk with Kendal, not learn what the three different sized forks were for.

I lowered my voice to her: "How you doing?"

She gave me a small smile. Her eyes were red like she'd been crying, but she looked better than when we flew here on the king's back.

"Better now that I'm not riding a dragon," she said sternly.

I nodded. "Hopefully, you don't have to do that again," I told her.

She grinned. "At least not in that way."

It took me a second to get her meaning and my mouth popped open at the dirty joke. Kendal was a wild card. Proper most days, encouraged others to stay pure, but she also knew the most about bedding a man than anyone else I knew. She claimed it was from visiting her aunt in Gypsy Rock, but now I wondered.

I bumped her shoulder with a smile. "Good one."

She burst into laughter and I found myself laughing too. I felt light and carefree for the first time since I'd gotten here.

Maybe this wouldn't be so bad.

The next few days passed slowly and I was ready to die of boredom. All the other girls wanted to talk about was sewing and flowers and how many children they wanted. Everyone seemed really excited to be here, and were anxious to meet the king and win his hand in marriage.

I on the other hand was anxious to hear about the war. We'd had little skirmishes now and again but not a full-on war for as long as I could remember. Last I'd heard from Narine was that the king and his army were holding the Nightfall queen and her men back at the Great River, but it had been an exhausting feat with more troops going out each day. Meanwhile, the prospective wives just kept getting up and wearing dresses and curling their hair, waiting for the king to arrive and choose one of them.

It was nauseating.

Speaking of nauseating: "I don't feel well. Please tell the other girls how much I will miss their company for lunch, but I think I'll stay in today," I told Narine.

I was half serious. I *didn't* feel well, but as sweet as they all were, I wouldn't miss the other girls' boring company. One more talk of the beautiful lilies in the garden and I was going to scream. Whenever I tried to tell a hunting story, they shushed me!

It just wasn't my preferred company.

Narine frowned, stepping forward to press a hand to my forehead, and then came away with a hiss. "I'll fetch a healer." She started to run from the room and I laughed.

"No, I'm fine. I just have a headache and need a nap," I mumbled, but the look of terror on her face made me wonder if I had spots on my skin or red cheeks. The pox took out a tenth of the village when I was little and I'd never had it before.

"You're burning up," was all she said, and then she slipped out the door.

I stumbled over to my bed, suddenly feeling shaky, and reached up to touch my own forehead. I felt fine, but would a person with a fever feel hot to themselves?

I was just tired. So tired that my brain felt like it was on fire. I lay down, unsure how long it would take to fetch a healer, and scared by the sudden turn of events.

I drifted off to sleep, only to be shaken awake some-time later.

"Miss Novakson? I'm Dr. Elsie," a woman with bright green hair said as she leaned over me and touched my head with a metal spoon-like object.

Her eyes widened with alarm and she looked to Narine, who was standing nearby.

"Run a cool bath, add ice," the doctor said.

"Ice?" I hissed.

The doctor stared down at me with concern and my eyes went to the tips of her ears to see that sure enough, they were pointed.

Elf?

Elves were famous for their healing, unlike their fae brethren and dragons had a bit of healing magic as well. "Miss Nov—"

"Call me Arwen," I moaned, feeling a bead of sweat trickle down my neck. The slight icky feeling I'd had a few moments ago had given way to full-on illness. My stomach burned with heat and my head felt like someone was squeezing it.

"Arwen, I am an elf-dragon with a specialist degree in hybrid illnesses. I have both an advanced doctor degree in dragon-folk and human maladies, as well as schooling in elven healing."

Blah, blah, I was dying and she was rattling on about her qualifications. An elf-dragon hybrid? That was pretty rare—next to impossible, really. I'd never met one, but my brain was on fire and so in this moment I didn't really care.

"I'm so tired, it burns. Water," I mumbled, starting to feel delirious.

The woman leaned forward then and stuck her nose right up against my neck and inhaled. She reminded me of a damn sniffer, and it was beyond rude to invade someone's personal space like this.

"Hey!" I shoved her away, starting to see wavy lines rise up off of my body like you would see heat when it hit hot stone at mid-day.

What the...?

The doctor's eyes widened and she blinked at me repeatedly. "You don't smell like a hybrid," she breathed.

Oh Hades. My mother's words of warning rushed back to me.

"What?" I laughed it off, one hundred percent sure I was going to burst into flames any second. The heat was all-consuming.

"*And* you smell like you're covered in spell magic that's wearing off." She said it almost accusatorily.

"What!?" I shrieked.

I could see something wrestling behind her eyes—compassion and condemnation both in equal measure, as if it were somehow my fault that someone had put a spell on me at birth.

"Ice bath is ready!" Narine called out. The doctor shook herself, sliding one hand under my legs and another behind my neck.

She scooped me up, grunting under my weight, and rushed me across the room.

The smell of burning skin wafted through the air and I gagged, looking up at the doctor. She winced in pain as smoke singed up to the ceiling. Following the smoke, I peered down in horror to see that it was *her* skin that was burning. And *I* was the one burning her.

What the Hades? How was this possible?

"I'll walk," I said, but my words came out warbled, and black dots danced at the edges of my vision. When she reached the tub, she dropped me into it like a hot coal. My body crashed into the sharp icy coldness and a hiss of steam exploded outward and darkness pulled me into its sweet embrace.

My consciousness returned to the sound of murmuring voices.

"Why does the washroom look like a bomb went off?" The king's growly voice invaded my mind but I was too weak to open my eyes.

"My lord, I cannot explain it. She... *exploded* with power," Dr. Elsie said. "I've never seen so much dragon fire in my life. Luckily, Narine and I are partial dragon-folk or we would have burned alive. I was able to use my elf magic to shield us from most of the blast."

My heart raced with what I was hearing. Were they talking about *me*?

I finally managed to open my eyelids and peered down at the end of my bed. King Valdren stood with his arms crossed over his muscular chest. Dried cuts and scars littered his arms, and there was black charcoal along his neck. He was fresh from battle.

"What does it mean?" he asked the doctor. I closed my eyes in case they were going to look over at me. I too wanted to know what it meant. Last I remembered, I'd been burning up, literally, and then Dr. Elsie had dunked me into some water and I passed out.

When the doctor spoke, her voice was so soft I barely heard her. "My lord, she reeked of spellwork. As if someone had done a spell to conceal her powers and the spell suddenly fell away, unable to contain it anymore."

Hades. This was not good. Everything my mother had said was turning out to be true.

"Why would someone conceal her power?" he asked, dumbfounded.

"I do not know, but if you're looking for someone to carry a child for you... she should be a top contender." I heard her shuffle closer to him. "She smelled *pure-blooded.*"

I stiffened, feeling his eyes on me. My heart beat so

loud and so frantically that I was sure the entire room could hear it.

Top contender for royal womb?

No. That's not what I was supposed to be doing. My mother said to lay low and hurry home. Then I exploded with dragon fire in front of the king's personal physician and had just moved myself up to top rank.

"Pure-blooded isn't possible," he said dismissively.

"A healer elf's nose doesn't lie," she retorted.

"You're *half* elf." His voice held a dangerousness that scared me.

"Well, she's close to pure-blooded," the doctor amended. "I'm sure of that. Have the sniffers check her now to confirm it if you like."

A silence fell over the both of them, and then the king spoke barely above a whisper. "Do you really think she's powerful enough to carry and deliver a baby to term? I can't bury another child." The king's voice broke, and the icy wall I'd built around my heart melted in an instant.

The sorrow in his tone consumed me. I had to swallow a whimper.

"Let's let her rest," the doctor said suddenly, and I feared that I actually *had* whimpered. My eyes snapped open just in time to see her pulling him out of the room.

Once I heard the door shut, I rolled onto my side and stared at the gold-stamped dragon emblem wallpaper.

He was just a man who wanted a child, and his magic was so powerful that most women's bodies could not carry one for him. Would it be so bad if I were to? I wanted children eventually—but I wanted to fall in love *first* and then have a baby born out of that love. What this whole spectacle sounded like was that the king wanted the heir and not the woman. I wasn't signing up for that.

I just needed to pray that my magic stayed in my body for the rest of my time here and that he chose someone else to be his next queen. I wanted him to have his heir, just not with me, not in a competition. I wouldn't be a prize.

I fell back asleep with thoughts of Nathanial and the kissing tent. The way he looked at Ruby Ronaldson meant that even if I did go home, they'd already be engaged.

It took me two days to recover from my fever and accidental dragon explosion incident. I played dumb to the doctor, saying that I had no idea about any magic, and that as far as I knew I was a watered-down dragon-folk. Doctor Elsie and Narine had sustained some slight burns that had already healed, but all in all were okay. The washroom repairs would take a week, but in the meantime I could use the second guest washroom. Something rich people had.

The next morning I awoke to hear Narine whistling. My eyelids sprang open and I peered at her. She was bopping on her heels, hands behind her back.

"What?" I mumbled. Narine didn't display this sort of happiness for no reason.

"You have a lunch date with the king in a few hours!" she squealed.

I bolted upright, rubbing the sleep from my eyes. "What?"

Narine nodded. "And a dress has come for the occasion."

Oh, that's why she was excited.

I dipped my head. "Good. Take the dress and sell it before I've even worn it. I don't want to get anything on it."

She frowned. "But... my lady, you have only simple

day dresses not suitable for lunch with his royal highness."

I swung my legs over the side of the bed and stood, reaching my arms over my head to stretch. "His royal highness saw me kill a man while I rode on his back. He doesn't expect a lady. Fetch my trousers and tunic."

If it was lunch alone with him and not a big event with the other women, I wanted to be myself. I was worried it would be an interrogation about my heritage now that Dr. Elsie had told him she'd smelled a spell on me.

Narine swayed on her feet, grasping the window ledge as if she were going to faint. "My lady... you can't... wear *trousers* to have lunch with the king."

"I can and I will," I informed her. I wasn't going to be someone I was not for a man who might end up killing me if he found out about my magic.

No thanks.

Narine took a few steadying breaths. "This could look bad on me with Annabeth," she said.

I waved her off and walked out of the room into the washroom. "I'll tell her you are amazing and I forced you to allow me to wear my preferred clothes."

She let a small smile slip. "Do you even want to see the dress before I sell it?"

I started to brush my teeth and nodded. She left

the room and returned holding a silky pink and purple gown with hand-stitched flowers and frilly sleeves.

I spit into the washbasin and then looked at her. "It's beautiful."

It was. It would look amazing on Kendal.

She seemed hopeful, gesturing for me to take it.

"Sell it. I'll let you do my hair."

With a groan she nodded. "At least wear a corset over your tunic to accentuate your waist. Hiding that figure under baggy clothing won't land you a husband."

Thinking of my mother's advice to seduce the king if things looked like they might not be going in my favor made me realize Narine was right.

I nodded.

It was a good compromise.

A few hours later, I peered into the mirror with a smile.

I wore tight black suede hunting trousers, a royal blue silk tunic that was short and tight—nothing like I'd ever seen before—and a small black leather waist cincher that ended just under my bust. I made sure Narine didn't tie it tightly, and even did a squat to make sure I could move about easily.

She'd curled my hair and braided it over one shoulder. I even let her fuss over me with makeup.

"I think you may have just invented a new style." Narine stared at me, rubbing her chin. "I like it."

I put my hands on my small waist. "I love it." Reaching out, I slipped my hunting blade into a thigh holster on my waist and Narine shook her head.

"For lunch with the king! Are you mad?" She yanked the blade out and stashed it in a drawer nearby.

I spit out my tongue at her. She already had a buyer for the dress. Ten jade coins, sight unseen.

There was a knock at the door.

Narine answered it, and then looked at me, stricken. "It's Annabeth, here to take you to your lunch date."

I nodded, knowing she was worried how me not wearing the dress might look.

I walked into view of Annabeth and watched as her gaze ran over my outfit. "Don't you love my stylish trouser suit? I insisted on wearing it. I think it will be all the rage at court once I am queen," I said with a Jade City accent.

Annabeth shared a worried look with Narine.

"I tried to persuade her to wear the dress," Narine said nervously.

Annabeth stared at Narine with pity, and then at me. "It looks... like something Regina might wear."

I grinned. That was truly a compliment. "Thanks."

After wishing Narine a good day, Annabeth led me down a network of hallways to a smaller set of double doors. "The king's private dining hall," Annabeth said, and opened the door. She took one last look at my outfit and shook her head. "Good luck."

I tried not to let my nerves get the better of me. Had the king requested this lunch with me to probe about my magic? Or was he meeting all of the women privately to assess their wifeliness?

I stepped into the hall as she closed the doors behind me. Spinning around, I surveyed the room. It was covered in black plush carpet; the walls were black as well, with a gold dragon emblem print. It would have been too dark if not for the magnificent chandelier and giant open window facing the garden. It was masculine, and fitting for the dragon king.

In the center of the room was a small four-person dining table. I suddenly felt weird being here. Had he eaten here with Queen Amelia?

A *thwack* drew my attention to the window and I wandered over to peer outside. The king was shooting a bow and arrow in the garden.

Now *that* was what I called a date. I looked for the door that led outside to join him, but he stowed the bow and began walking towards me. The back doors to the room opened and a man stepped in rolling a food cart.

"Oh, hey." I walked over to the table but didn't yet sit down. I didn't want to sit in the king's favorite chair or anything.

A second later, the man of the hour stepped inside. He wore a nice black silk dress tunic that fell past his knees, and suede trousers much like mine. His gaze landed on me and did a slow inventory of my body, before a halfcocked smile dragged across his lips.

"Did Annabeth see you dressed like that?" he asked.

I nodded. "She loved it," I lied, knowing he could smell it.

"Liar."

I grinned. Okay, he was in a joking mood. This was good.

"Thank you, Ferlin," the king told the man who had set two plates full of warm food at the table.

"Ladies first," the king said, gesturing to the table-sitting closest to me. I nodded, taking my seat, and pulled my napkin onto my lap.

Ferlin wheeled his cart out and I looked at the delicious plate before me. Crab, potatoes, and some kind of green salad.

"I'm starved. I skipped breakfast," I informed him

and grabbed my fork, digging into the deliciousness. I made sure to take small bites and chew slowly so that he didn't think me a total pigin, but still he seemed to watch me with careful eyes.

He reached over and grasped his fork, pretending to write on the table. "Refuses to wear dresses, eats like a starved child... anything else I should know?" he asked, half smiling.

I had to hold in my shocked laughter. *The king is funny.* I liked seeing this side of him. I grabbed my fork and mimicked him by pretending to write on the table.

"Is currently dating a hundred women at once, only wants me for my womb." I gave him a challenging smirk.

His eyes absolutely glittered with mirth at my jab.

He pretended to scribble on the table again. "Can take a joke and hit back with one."

I laughed. "I didn't take you for a funny guy."

He shrugged. "You're different than the others. I like that. I feel I can be relaxed around you."

It was a very sweet thing to say. It made me wonder if he had people in his life that he felt he couldn't be himself around.

"I do not covet the dresses and flowers and makeup as much as the other women, that's true." I nodded.

He took a bite of his food. "Are you enjoying the crab? Have you ever had it before?"

"It's wonderful. I've only had crab one other time, on a visit to Jade City a few years ago."

He looked surprised at that. "You've been to Jade City before?"

I nodded. "Back when Queen Amelia was—for the royal wedding." I stopped myself, realizing what I'd done. "I had a wonderful time." I left it at that, regretting saying her name, unsure how painful it was for him to hear.

He gave me a wan smile, taking a bite of his own food, but a darkness had cast itself over our meal. It was silent for a moment and I felt awful.

"I'm sorry for bringing her up. I wasn't thinking," I finally said.

He waved me off. "It's fine. I just miss her. She was my best friend."

"How long had you known her before you got married?" I asked, wondering if asking these questions was okay.

He swallowed hard. "It's not a well-known thing, so please keep this private, but Amelia and I were betrothed at birth by our parents."

I gasped. "Betrothed at birth? You always knew you were going to marry her?"

He nodded. "Always."

An arranged marriage. They were more common with the fae than here but they did happen. Still, I wasn't sure how I would feel knowing my whole life had been mapped out for me. He'd called her his best friend, but did that mean that's all they were? Or was there a romantic love too? My tongue burned with unasked questions that I forced myself to swallow down.

"So when did you start hunting?" He changed the subject and I was grateful.

I swallowed hard, the lump of crab falling into my stomach like a stone. "After my father died. I was nine."

His hand stilled. "The men in your village didn't help out your family? I thought the Cinder community was close?"

I nodded. "We are. They helped as long as they could, but with my little sister there are three mouths to feed, and my mom didn't want to remarry just for food. So I took on the responsibility. Kept us fed."

His hand reached out, draping over mine, and heat pooled in my belly as I looked up into his sincere green eyes. "That's incredibly admirable of you, Arwen."

It was as if all the oxygen had been sucked from the room. His hand on mine caused my chest to heave. He must have realized the effect his touch had on me, because he yanked it back a second later.

"So have you been feeling well? No more fevers?" He changed the subject again. He seemed to be an expert at that.

I picked at my dinner roll, no longer trusting my body to stick with the plan.

What was the plan? Oh yeah, don't fall for the king! He didn't want love, he wanted my magical womb, and might kill me if he found out who my birth mother was. Yet I couldn't help but admit I'd judged him wrong. He was not what I thought. "Nope. All good."

"Did you know you had a spell on you to keep your powers hidden?" he asked nonchalantly, but I saw his body stiffen. He didn't fully trust me, and he could smell a lie, so I had to be careful.

I shook my head. "I had nothing to do with any spell put on me." It was the truth, but didn't fully answer his question.

He seemed pleased with that answer. "I'll need to teach you to control your powers as they fully come forward. You don't want to get angry and breathe fire all over someone."

My eyes widened. "You think I can breathe fire?" I was genuinely shocked to think of being capable of such a thing.

He shrugged. "It's possible. Over the next few days I'll have you work with myself or Regina to see."

I shrank into myself, suddenly uncomfortable with him trying to get me to display my power. "I... don't know how I feel about that. I've never displayed dragon magic before."

He waved me off. "Whenever you're ready."

Relief rushed through me and we settled into an easy conversation. What my biggest animal kill was, what his was, our favorite weapon.

"I'm a fan of the bow." I tipped my head outside to where he had been practicing.

"I prefer a spear," he said, finishing his last bite of crab.

He followed my gaze to the archery set-up outside. "Do you want to have a go?"

I stood eagerly. "I thought you'd never ask."

He shook his head with a smile, and then indicated I follow him outside. Once we were on the lawn, he handed me a medium sized bow. I recognized the elven gold immediately.

"Gift from the elf king when I was a teenager," he told me. "It should be about your size."

I lowered the bow and reached out to hand it back to him. "I shouldn't use such a special gift."

He waved me off. "It fits you," was all he said before he took a larger bow of his own.

I let my fingers trail the smooth alder wood, running my fingertips over the filigree engraving on the gold. Plucking an arrow from the basket, I set the notch into the string and pulled it a few times to test the tightness and get a feel for the weapon.

I could feel the king watching me as I raised the bow up and locked my elbow, drawing the string back. I lined it up with the center dot on the wooden target and took in a deep breath. I readjusted my aim and then held my breath, releasing the arrow.

It sailed through the air and sliced into the wood with a *thwack*.

Right on the dot.

I glanced over at the king and he nodded. "Impressive."

I stepped to the side and then he strode up to the shooter's position.

He pulled one arrow, barely took a half second to line it up, and then released it. It landed an inch above mine. Before I could comment, he grabbed another arrow, released it, another and another. Within thirty seconds he'd loosed half a dozen arrows and drawn a circle around mine in the center.

When he looked back at me with a smirk, I rolled my eyes.

"Showoff."

Deep throaty laughter erupted from him and it warmed my belly. "Would this be a date without a little showing off?" he asked.

A date. He called it a date. My whole body coiled in response to the word. I suddenly wasn't so mad about being in the running to be his wife. Would it be so bad? He seemed like a nice guy, he was handsome, funny, and a good shot with a bow. I did find myself wondering if he had asked me to lunch because Dr. Elsie had told him I was one of his best shots to getting an heir. I didn't want to be chosen for my child-bearing abilities.

"It's not a proper date unless I get dessert," I added playfully.

He tipped his head in agreement. "To the kitchens."

"I feel a bit sick... but I can't stop!" I exclaimed an hour later.

The king watched me lick melted chocolate off my fork and his eyes hooded as I swiped my tongue out again to get the last crumb of cake from the utensil.

We were sitting at a small table in the kitchen, and the Jade Castle chef had just given us an entire chocolate raspberry cake to share with two forks.

I looked at the king quizzically, enjoying this day that we'd had together. It wasn't what I had expected— and to be honest I wanted more of it. "What's the grossest thing you've ever eaten?"

He scrunched up his face at my question. "Ratin."

"No way you've eaten ratin!" I pointed to him. "Liar."

He smiled easily, something he seemed to do a lot of in my presence. His teeth were bright white and straight. When he smiled hugely there was a slight dimple in his right cheek. "I have. The Drayken and I were stuck in a cave for three days fighting off the Nightfall queen two summers back. They tried to starve us out."

Wow, I hadn't thought his royal highness would eat ratin, but he was a warrior too, so it made sense.

"Ratin was the first kill I brought home after my father died," I told him.

His face took on a somber mood and he nodded. "The pangs of hunger are not picky, I have learned."

I dipped my chin. "They are not."

145

He looked into my eyes then and a conflicted feeling came over me. I'd be lying if I said I didn't enjoy his company. I didn't like the sense of duty providing an heir entailed but I couldn't lie to myself anymore... I liked him.

He reached out and grasped a stray lock of my blond hair, tucking it behind my ear, and chills ran the length of my back. His hand stilled and he stroked two fingers across my cheek. My eyelids fluttered closed and the door burst open, causing both of us to jump. The king yanked his hand back and my eyelids snapped open.

"My lord, we have an emergency in Grim Hollow," a guard said.

The king took one more look at me. "Thank you for meeting me, Arwen."

I nodded, still feeling him tracing my cheek even though he was no longer touching me. I wanted to thank him too and to ask him what was going on in Grim Hollow, but by the time my wits returned to me, he was gone and I was left feeling all kinds of confused.

Tonight was the first night I would dress up for a welcome ball and meet the king "officially." I hadn't heard from him since our date a few nights ago. I was hoping there wouldn't be so many women there tonight that it would leave him no time to talk with me. All I'd thought about the past two days were of the sensation on my cheek when his fingers had trailed across it.

"Your dress has arrived!" Narine trilled from the entryway as an assistant to the seamstress walked in carrying the most beautiful emerald-green dress I'd ever seen. It glittered in the light, with a tight corset bust and a waist that looked like a bell.

It was fit for a *queen*.

I had made a compromise with Narine. During the big balls with all the other girls, I would wear dresses, but if it were a date or just me walking around the palace, I was in trousers.

"Holy Hades!" I gawked at the gown as the seamstress laid it on the couch and then bowed to me before leaving.

I turned to Narine. "You'll get good money for this, right?"

She grinned. "I already have a buyer for twenty jade coins."

Each day I was supplied with new clothing as if wearing the same thing twice was a crime. A few of the cotton day dresses I kept for my mother and Adaline. I liked my trousers and silk tunics. The seamstress had sewn me four pairs, and I wore them whenever appropriate to not be in a dress.

"I'll be sure not to spill anything on it," I promised her.

She looked at me then with a seriousness in her gaze. "I will never forget this kindness. At this rate, I'll have my sister's wedding paid off by next moon!"

I gave her a genuine smile. "Let's try it on!"

I'd never been overly into fashion but I didn't mind looking like a queen for a few hours. I was going to enjoy this time here at Jade City so that when I went back home I would have a lot of fun memories to go back with.

The thought of going home now, after my date with the king, made a pang of sadness creep into my heart.

"I've been practicing my braiding on Mida, another maid. I have this idea I want to try with your hair and some jade stones I was able to get from the royal jeweler." She dug into her pocket and pulled out a pouch.

"Sounds fun! Do whatever," I told her as she unzipped the back of the dress.

I slipped out of my clothes, now comfortable with Narine seeing me naked, as she had bathed me many times now. Narine had me raise my arms over my head, and then slipped the dress over my small frame. The inside was lined with silk, so the glittery fabric didn't itch.

"Deep breath in," Narine said.

I frowned. "Why?"

She pulled the string to the corset and suddenly my rib cage was squeezed. "Ahh." I sucked in a deep breath to widen my chest and she loosened it a bit, laughing.

"You enjoyed that," I sniped at her playfully.

"Just a little."

After dressing me, she made me promise not to look in the mirror, and then brought me an old book to read while she went to work on my hair.

I was a slow reader, never had much opportunity to read full novels, but by the time she was done with my hair I'd read six chapters of a gripping fantasy about a wolf shifter and a shadow demon who fell in love.

"Who wrote this?" I asked, looking at the leather cover.

The letters J.E. were embossed in gold.

"She lives in town, a highborn," Narine said, and then tapped my shoulders. "Ready to look?"

I set the book face-down so that I could pick back up where I left off, and nodded.

Stepping over to the mirror, I had to walk slowly so that I didn't trip. When I faced myself, I startled for a second, not recognizing the woman before me.

"I'm so clean," I exclaimed, never having seen my skin and fingernails and hair so spotless in all my life.

She laughed. "You're more than that. You're beautiful."

I really took myself in, then gasped when I saw the

lattice-like pattern she'd somehow managed with my hair. It was like a net had been braided over my ponytail and then small jewels glittered throughout.

"You're an artist!" I exclaimed.

Narine blushed. "Hardly. I just like to be creative."

I rolled my eyes. "That's what artists do."

After applying some light makeup, we set off for the main ballroom, where our dinner was to be served.

Each and every girl I walked by complimented my hair, and every time Narine beamed with pride. Kendal wore a truly stunning red gown that complemented her hair, and we sat together and talked immediately. The girls had heard I'd had some sort of illness a few days ago but not what it was.

"Is your fever better?" asked Joslyn, the girl from Grim Hollow.

She and Kendal seemed to have formed a friendship. Tonight she wore a bright gold gown with black beading, which complemented her bronze skin tone and dark hair.

I smiled. "Yes, thank you."

Murmurs rose up, and I peered at the front of the room to see that the king had entered. He looked devastatingly handsome in his black leather Royal Guard uniform. His eyes scanned the crowd eagerly, and then stopped on me.

My back went rigid as his pupils glowed yellow for a split second. Leaning over, he whispered something to Regina, who stood next to him, and she nodded and then left.

I swallowed hard, unsure if he'd said something about me or not. It certainly looked like he had.

"I'm sorry I've been absent the past few days." His voice boomed throughout the room and everyone fell silent. "We had a skirmish at our border, which has now been taken care of and secured."

The room made a collective sigh at that news and then he went on.

"As much as I would like to get to know each one of you personally and make my decision for a new wife based on compatibility..." He paused. "That will not achieve the outcome I desire, which is a healthy heir."

Everyone went dead silent. His openness was not expected, at least not from me.

"I would like you all to enjoy your meal. We will be pulling you out in groups of five to test your magic. If you cannot produce enough dragon-folk magic to my physicians' liking, you will be sent home early with payment as promised for the full month."

The room erupted into shocked gasps and whispers. Kendal, Joslyn, and I traded a wary glance. The king was clearly in a hurry, and a lot of the girls were having fun playing dress-up, but it seemed that fun was over. I was torn about whether or not I wanted to manifest enough magic during my test to keep me here. He'd just said that I'd be getting the five hundred jade coins whether I stayed the full month or not. I'd give some to Narine to help with her sister's wedding and I'd take the rest to my mother. But... did I want to be sent home? To never see him again? Or worse, watch him marry another? It might be better than the alternative. To manifest so much magic that he found out who I really was. A pure-blood that apparently had magic that could harm him. Wasn't that what my mother had said?

After spending time with the king, I was certain now that he wouldn't hurt me if he found out who I was.

Right?

I t was a beautiful night. One I would cherish forever. It was how I imagined a big highborn wedding would be like. There was a four string musical ensemble, an endless buffet of food, dancing... it was magical. All except for Regina pulling groups of five girls out, and only one, or in some cases none, coming back. The room was starting to thin, and Kendal and I could no longer stomach dancing. The nervous anticipation of what was to come had us all on edge.

"What do you think the test is?" I asked, but Joslyn shushed me.

"Enjoying yourselves, ladies?" the king's voice boomed behind me and I went rigid.

"Oh yes," Joslyn cooed up at him.

"Such a lovely evening," Kendal told him.

"And you, Arwen?" he asked me.

I spun in my seat and pointed to my empty plate. "The food is divine."

"Would you dance with me?" he asked, holding his hand out to me.

I froze, immediately starting to sweat. *Dance with him? Why?* He hadn't danced with anyone else.

I looked at Kendal, who widened her eyes as if saying you did *not* reject a dance with the king.

I stood. "Uh, sure, but I warn you I tend to step on toes." I took his outstretched hand and allowed him to bring me to the dance floor, my mind running wild.

He watched me curiously, then his gaze fell to my lips. I swallowed hard to wet my throat. Wild and free dancing with Kendal was one thing, but slow dancing with the king of Embergate was another story.

He placed a hand on my lower back and took my palm into his as we slowly rocked back and forth to the music. I struggled to breathe this close to him, his body lightly pressed against mine. I could feel the entire room's eyes on me, and yet it felt so right. It felt like I was made to be in his arms and I didn't want to let him go.

Leaning into my ear, he said, "You look breathtaking."

My stomach heated at the compliment.

"Thank you. How did the issue at Grim Hollow go?" I asked.

He peered down at me. "It was the Nightfall queen. I lost some men, but they lost more."

That was a relief.

"Tell me about your parents," he asked suddenly.

I stiffened a little, but then smiled to cover my nervousness. "My father worked in the Cinder mine. He would go drink at the tavern every weekend, and that's where he met my mom. She was the barmaid."

He looked at me coolly, as if testing my response for lies more than actually having an interest in what I was saying. "And your father was a quarter dragon-folk you said?"

I dropped his hand and stepped back as if I'd been burned. "Are you interrogating me or getting to know me?" I snapped, causing a few nearby girls to turn in our direction.

Redness crept up his cheeks and he stepped closer

to me, taking me back into his arms, this time more forcefully than before.

He pressed his hand into my lower back, my stomach going flush up against his. He leaned into my neck, whispering into my ear: "I'm trying to find out how a girl who claims to be a quarter dragon-folk explodes like a magic bomb in one of my washrooms. A girl I very much like and am interested in."

Chills ran down my spine at the accusation in his tone, but also at the hot breath that rushed down my neck and the declaration that he liked me.

Still, I couldn't help the anger that rose up inside of me at his mistrust, and I peered back to look at him. "Why don't you answer a few questions for me?"

His eyes flashed from green to yellow.

"What would make you seek an heir so badly that you would court a hundred ladies at once, when your wife has barely been gone a winter?"

His face fell into a mask of horror and I instantly regretted my words. His hands dropped from my back and he took a giant step away from me.

"My lord, I'm sorry—"

He waved me off and turned, leaving the room, and I prayed to the Maker to be swallowed up into a giant hole rather than to ever have to see him again after saying such a hurtful thing. Why did I do that?

Fear. I feared that if he liked me, it meant I might actually be in the running to be his wife, and if my mother's warning was real... I needed to avoid that at all costs.

I sulked all the way back to my seat, where Joslyn and Kendal peered over at me intently.

"Well, what was said?" Kendal asked. "He looked hurt when he walked off."

I shook my head, indicating I didn't want to talk about it, and grabbed my plate. I was going to eat two more slices of cake. That way, when the king sent me home, my belly would be full.

The night began to drag on. I just wanted to go back to my room and sleep. But it seemed Regina was Hades-bent on picking me last. When she finally entered the room and waved Kendal, Joslyn, and I over, I sighed in relief. I just wanted to get this over with and fall into a chocolate-cake food-coma. I was regretting that third slice.

Standing up with the other girls, I walked on shaky legs over to the side door that Regina was waiting for us at.

She looked as tired as I felt. It must be near

midnight, but it was clear there was an urgency to find the king's next wife, so they were rushing this process along. It didn't matter to me. After what I'd said to him, I would be lucky if he didn't hang me in the village square.

Regina gave us three a tight smile, and then inclined her head for us to follow her.

Did the king tell her what I'd said to him? If so, I was mortified. Who spoke to royalty like that? What was wrong with me? The worst part was that I liked him. I said something horrible to someone I liked and now I felt like crap.

We followed Regina down a long hallway to another set of double doors.

I'd built up such a ball of nerves that when she pulled them open to reveal the king standing at the back of the room, I yelped a little.

All three pairs of eyes fell upon me and I swallowed hard.

"Thought I saw a spider," I explained.

Calm down, Arwen. This is going to be totally fine.

We entered the room and I balked at the size of the crowd. There were half a dozen sniffers, a handful of Royal Guards, Dr. Elsie, and some old dude holding a leather-bound tome. They all stood at the outer edges of the walls. In the center of the room was a single icy blue crystal that sat on a small white stone pedestal. I inhaled, the smell of smoke hitting my nostrils, and then I noticed the scorch marks.

Black streaks fanned out across the white jade stone tile leading out from the crystal.

"Kendal, please step forward and touch the Revealing Stone," Regina said, and Kendal looked at me with fear.

Going first sucked.

I gave her a supportive nod, while my mind chewed on the words. *Revealing stone.* Did it reveal the extent of our power? I sure as Hades hoped not. Especially not after my spell had fallen off, or whatever that washroom explosion and fever was.

The older gentleman with the leather book opened it to a particular page and then watched Kendal with a keen eye. Meanwhile, the sniffers tipped their chins up and flared their nostrils, as if waiting to get a whiff of magic.

The entire thing was creepy as all Hades. I wanted to run. I thought the sniffers coming to my village was the extent of the magical testing. This felt so much more intrusive.

Every caution my mother gave me was going off like a warning trumpet in my head.

Run. Run. Run.

As if sensing my panic, Regina stepped up behind me and I stood there frozen, nowhere to go.

Kendal's heels clacked across the floor as she walked over to the stone and stopped before it. Looking to the king, she held out her hands. "I just touch it?"

King Valdren looked tired. "Yes. The stone will bring forth a more potent example of your power so that we can assess your ability to carry a dragon-shifting child."

His voice was so monotone. It was clear he wasn't enjoying this at all.

Kendal chewed on her bottom lip and then grasped the stone. Orange flames burst from her hands in a two-foot circumference and I gasped. Kendal had *never* shown that much magic before. This stone really must push your power to its limits.

That scared the life out of me. If I'd exploded in the washroom, what would this stone make me do?

Kendal looked back at me with pride and I gave her a thumbs-up, but I also caught the king looking at Dr. Elsie, and the elf-dragon shook her head.

Regina stepped forward with a frown. "Thank you, Kendal. Follow me."

Wait... why did the doctor shake her head? Did that mean Kendal was going home? I wanted to ask, but I'd pushed my luck tonight when I'd told the king he was marrying too soon after his beloved wife's death.

Regina reappeared, and I wondered where she'd taken Kendal.

"Joslyn." She motioned her forward, and I pushed all worries about Kendal behind me.

They were saving me for last! That was just mean. I wanted to get this stupid thing over with. Joslyn walked forward with a confident smile and without hesitation grasped the blue stone before her.

An inferno of six-foot-tall orange flames shot up towards the ceiling and everyone stepped back a pace as they *oohed* and *ahhed*.

My gaze flicked to the king, who was appraising Joslyn, his eyes roaming over her body more closely than ever before.

He glanced at Dr. Elsie, who nodded enthusiastically.

Regina looked relieved as she stepped forward and ushered Joslyn out of the room. When she returned, all eyes went to me.

Hades. I don't want to do this.

Dr. Elsie leaned into the king's ear and whispered something. He stared at her with surprise before clearing his throat.

"Would everyone take five big steps back please,"

he commanded, and they looked at him with disbelief, including me.

Did Dr. Elsie think I was going to explode again? Like in the washroom? Because that was just a one-time thing as the spell to hide my power fell away... right?

They were already towards the back of the room. Now they pushed farther away from me, until their heels hit the far wall. It was laughable that my magic might travel that far.

"We're all very tired, Miss Novakson. Please get on with it." The king's voice was clipped, and shame burned my cheeks. I wanted to apologize for what I said on the dance floor but now wasn't the time. Taking small, tentative steps towards the stone, I tried to delay the inevitable. All the while, my mother's advice rang in my mind.

If it looks like he is going to find out about your powers, make him fall in love with you.

My gaze flicked to the king, who was glaring at me like he couldn't wait to send me home, and I sighed.

Love might no longer be in the cards; I'd screwed that up already. Maybe he'd still let me in his Royal Guard?

No chance.

As I neared the stone, the hairs on my arms stood

up and my breathing slowed. It was almost like I was walking through water or sand. The air was thick with power; it got harder and harder to breathe the closer I got. Did the other girls feel this too? If so, they didn't show it.

I reached my fingers out. Inches from the stone, a foreboding feeling came over me. Every cell in my body was telling me to run. The only other time I'd gotten this feeling was right before I'd been chased three miles downriver by a giant black bearin.

I hesitated, looking up at the king to see him watching me with suspicion. My gaze then danced to Regina, whose eyes narrowed. If I refused, would they attack me? Would they force me? For the first time since I agreed to this whole thing, I became scared.

I have to do this. Now I wished I'd done what my mother told me and made the king want my body, because nothing would save me now if this thing showed where my true lineage came from.

Maker protect me, I prayed, and grabbed the stone.

I knew the second it touched my skin that I'd made a horrible mistake.

Pure unearthly power ripped through my entire body and I was consumed with blue flames. Heat engulfed my skin as the blue fire burst outward and the room filled with screams. Pain tore across my shoulders as something had yanked me from behind.

I staggered backwards, the flames receding, and I peered over my shoulder to see who was dragging me backwards. When I saw two blue dragon wings, I gasped. Looking around the room, I sought King Valdren's gaze.

The king stared at me with absolute shock. The old man holding the leather-bound tome ran over to him and whispered frantically into his ear. I started to weep, scared of what was happening, what this all meant, and Dr. Elsie rushed towards me.

"No!" The king reached out, blocking Dr. Elsie, and then looked at his guards. "Seize her," he said.

What?

"My lord?" Regina sounded confused, and her guards hesitated.

"SEIZE HER!" King Valdren bellowed, and smoke curled from his nostrils.

The betrayal and shock of what he said sliced through my heart.

Two guards rushed forward, hooking arms under my armpits as I continued to sob and shake in fear.

What was happening? How were there wings on my back? Why was my fire blue and not orange like all of the other dragon-folk?

"My lord, she's scared. She doesn't know what this means," Dr. Elsie pleaded with him.

I peered up at him, begging for mercy with my gaze, but he just glared at me. "The first thing she ever told me was a lie. I can't trust her now."

I'd been kidding myself until now that my lunch date with him might have made him go easy on me. He looked like he wanted to burn me alive.

The guards dragged me away and I didn't bother correcting him. He was right.

I lay on the small bedroll inside the cell beneath the castle. Gone were the pretty jade palace walls with gold inlay. Now I was surrounded by gray, flat, damp, rock. No more chocolate cake and fancy balls, I'd spent that last twenty-four hours relieving myself into a bedpan while wearing this ridiculous dress, which was now ruined. The blue dragon wings that had sprung from my back had sucked back in by the time the guards brought me downstairs. Regina had visited me briefly to tell me that the king was investigating me for treason.

She'd looked regretful about having to even say those words, and then she'd left. The first twelve hours, I'd cried, full of fear. Then my tears dried and made way for anger. Now I was ready to kill someone.

How. Dare. He?

I simply make an offhanded comment about him marrying too soon, then I sprout wings and suddenly I'm treasonous?

If what my mother said was true, that my magic was a threat to him, then it wasn't my fault and there was nothing I could do. I would no longer cower and snivel before him. When he marched me into the city square for sentencing, I would not shed a tear *nor* bow my head.

I would *not* apologize for being born.

The sound of footsteps down the hall drew my attention. Another food tray delivery? Or maybe Regina here to tell me my fate?

I stood, brushing off my dusty gown, and tipped my chin up with pride.

When the king himself came into view in front of my bars, I couldn't help the small growl that ripped from my throat.

He swallowed hard, assessing me, his eyes raking

over my hair and then falling to my disheveled dress and bare feet.

"I'd like to question you. If you tell me the truth and do not lie, not even *once*, I will let you live."

"Let me *live*?" I shouted like a feral catin. "What could I possibly have done to deserve death?"

His eyes narrowed and he assessed me more closely. Looking to his right, at someone I could not see, he nodded. "Open the doors."

My heart hammered in my chest as Regina stepped into view and unlocked the door.

"Clean up and then meet me in my office. Remember, I require the truth from you, Arwen," he declared, and then left, his boots clacking down the hallway as he went.

Regina was then followed by two guards, and behind them my personal maid, Narine.

I couldn't help the tears that lined my eyes when I saw her. She rushed forward to hug me.

"I'm so sorry I got the dress dirty," I whispered in her ear.

She pulled back and looked at me in shock. "I don't care about the dress. Are you okay?"

"Come on, you can chat while she bathes," Regina said, urging us along and casting a glance in the direction of the guards.

I nodded, and followed Narine through a network of stairs and corridors until we were back in my room, with the two guards posted outside. Regina stayed in the living room, and Narine and I slipped into the washroom.

The moment we were alone, I felt a cascade of emotions overwhelm me. "Is Kendal okay?"

Narine nodded. "They sent her and most of the other girls back home today with a bag of coin and extra food. She's on a carriage to Cinder Village."

That was a relief. "Does she know about what happened to me?"

Narine shook her head. "I was told to tell everyone you were under the weather. Another fever."

That was good. I didn't want her telling my mother. While Narine ran my bathwater, we both worked to undo the beautiful lattice hair design she'd done, setting the jewels on the counter to be returned to the palace jeweler.

She was silent an entire minute before finally asking, "My lady... what happened? *Treason?*"

Right. They hadn't told her. Of course not.

I shrugged my shoulders. "I made a comment about marrying too soon after his wife's death and then I took some magical test where blue dragon wings popped from my back and he imprisoned me."

Her entire form went stock still. "You *transformed?*"

"I guess. Not really—just wings and not on purpose!" I promised.

She hadn't moved. Her hands were frozen over my hair and she just looked at me with an expression of complete wonderment. "Only full-blooded royals transform."

Full-blooded royals.

My mother had said that the woman who gave birth to me was a highborn, but she wasn't royal, right? That would make her a queen, and at the time of my birth the only queen alive was King Valdren's mother, who surely did not run off and have a secret child and die in childbirth.

Oh Hades, if I was King Valdren's long-lost sister, I would vomit right now.

Narine seemed to read my thoughts by the confused look on my face. She coaxed me over to the bath and then helped me undress.

"You've heard of the Lost Royal, right?" she asked, her voice barely a whisper.

Lost Royal?

I shook my head, unsure if the sudden goosebumps on my arms were from her story or my nakedness. I stepped into the warm bath, unable to truly enjoy it with my life on the line.

Narine started to wash my hair.

"A few centuries ago, there were *two* royal dragon families. Embergate was also broken up into two territories, with each royal family encompassing one part of it. Grim Hollow and Jade City used to be home of the Dark Night Dragon clan, which is what King Valdren is. And Gypsy Rock and Cinder Mountain were the Eclipse Dragon clan."

Eclipse Dragon clan?

Why had I never heard this story? Probably because it was something from some fancy history book that we didn't get in Cinder Village. But still, you would think it would be told verbally. "I've never heard this," I informed her.

She nodded. "It's forbidden to speak about. My mother told me when I was a young child."

Forbidden to speak of a story? That didn't sound right.

"What happened to the other royal family?" I really, *really*, didn't want to know the answer to that question, but I asked it anyway.

She looked at the door, the one that Regina sat on the other side of. "The queen of the Eclipse Dragons went to war with the Dark Night Dragon clan and slaughtered nearly all of them. For what reason, I don't know."

I could physically feel the blood draining from my face. "Eclipse Dragon queen?"

She nodded. "The queen of Cinder Mountain. She had a special type of magic. They called her the *king killer*. She could steal other dragon-folks' magic and merge it with hers, making her all-powerful."

My heart must have stopped, because I didn't feel it anymore. I just felt... numb... and in shock. So very much in shock that I forgot to breathe for a moment.

No. Make it not true. *Make it a lie*, I prayed.

Narine went on, speaking barely above a whisper. "When the Eclipse Dragon queen tried to kill the Dark Night Dragon king, who at the time was King Valdren's great-great grandfather, she lost. But it's said her daughter went into hiding in the cliffs above Gypsy Rock with her husband and that the royal line lived on."

My heart hammered in my chest. "What are you saying?"

Narine chewed her bottom lip and faced me. "I'm saying, my lady, that I think you are the lost queen of the Eclipse Dragon clan."

My heart fell into my stomach and I couldn't

speak. How? It wasn't possible. A queen? That was a joke.

I shook my head and laughed nervously. "A good children's story surely," I murmured. "Besides, I only transformed my wings."

Her eyes cast downward to the floor. "This time," she mumbled.

What did *that* mean? That next time I would *fully* transform? I couldn't handle this anymore. In an effort to escape the conversation, I slid down and dunked my soapy head underwater.

The memory of the blue wings hanging off my back came to my mind and I considered Narine's story. It sort of lined up with my mother's. That the woman who gave birth to me had fled a battle, covered in blood, and said that her entire family had been killed, right? Maybe eighteen winters ago, when I was born, the dragon king at the time had found her in hiding and killed them all. I tried to remember every word my mother had said, but I'd been under stress and the exact wording of the story failed me.

Two things I did remember...

The woman who birthed me had said her family was killed because of a magic they carried.

And she'd said I would be killed if that magic were revealed in me.

I would need air soon, but I didn't want to leave the water and the safety of its embrace. I lingered another moment, then I broke the top of the water and gasped, relieved to see that Narine had left me to myself. Clean clothes lay folded on the chair in front of the window.

This might be the last bath I ever took. King Valdren did me a small kindness in letting me clean up before my interrogation, but I knew what I was about to walk into. The king could smell a lie, and so this interrogation was going to be a truth bomb of epic proportions that would no doubt get me killed.

I only had one thing he desired, and that was my womb, so I needed to hope like Hades that he really wanted an heir that badly, and promote my child-rearing powers lest my life end today.

It was time to take my mother's advice and make him fall in love with me. Whether it was possible or not.

When I stepped out of the washroom, Narine looked right at my unbuttoned tunic and a slight smirk graced her lips. I'd left it open just enough to give a hint of my cleavage. I also kept my hair down in loose waves, as I had heard men at the tavern say they liked that once. I wasn't proud of what I was doing, but I was desperate enough to do it. I needed the king to see me as more than a threat, which was all I was to him now.

A king killer.

Especially after hearing Narine's story. If that was true, and my great-great grandmother nearly killed off all of his clan, then I was in grave danger.

I waved goodbye to Narine and she gave me an anxious smile of encouragement. Regina stood, her face devoid of all emotion as she gestured for me to walk with her. I needed allies if I was going to save my life, and Regina had been kind to me before.

"Treason for having wings? How is that possible? I didn't even know I could do that until he put me through that test," I told her as we left my rooms.

She kept her head forward and said nothing.

"Did he tell you what I did at Gypsy Rock? That I rode on his back and killed a warrior from Nightfall? I protected him!" I yelled.

She stopped, turning to face me, and my heart hammered in my throat.

"I've fought beside the king in many battles. He is a just man who does not make irrational decisions. I trust that he has his reasons for your... treatment." She then resumed walking.

Okay, that wasn't exactly a declaration of becoming my ally, but I would take it.

It was a long walk to the torture room or whatever place they were taking me. We passed a library, kitchens, two training rooms, and finally made it to a set of double doors.

I released a shaky breath as Regina reached out and knocked.

I turned to her, suddenly desperate. "If he kills me, tell my mother and Adaline that I love them."

She looked stricken, as if the idea that the king would kill me was preposterous. But I was just imprisoned for the last twenty-four hours and now I was being questioned for treason, so she nodded, and then the door opened.

The king stood there in full battle armor, his jaw clenched. "Thank you, Regina. You may wait out here."

She nodded. "Yes, my lord."

He opened the door wide. Behind him, I saw a single chair sitting in the middle of the room. A small whimper escaped me and I swallowed it down, stepping inside. The door closed behind me and I peered around wildly. There were no windows, only four sconces on the walls that burned with orange dragon fire.

"Sit," he commanded, and I swallowed hard, taking my seat.

I looked up to face him and he walked towards me, his face bathed in the orange glow of the flames. He didn't look as mad as I expected, more curious.

When his eyes fell to my open tunic, I couldn't help but feel a small internal victory. Stepping right up to me, he reached out and I stilled. Grasping my tunic, he began to button it up.

"Nice try, but it will take more than a beautiful woman to distract me," he said, and then dropped the shirt back down to my chest.

My cheeks burned with embarrassment. He knew what my plan was?

Did he just call me *beautiful*?

"Let's get this over with. I've done nothing wrong." I crossed my arms and glared at him. I would never forget that he'd made me use a bed pan over the last twenty-four hours like a sick patient!

He stood before me, towering over me.

"I'll determine that." His eyes flashed yellow. "Now, tell me everything you know about your power, and if you do not lie I may be able to repair my broken trust with you."

Broken trust? I barely knew him.

I scowled at him. "Why don't you tell me all of

your hidden secrets as well, so that *you* can earn *my* trust."

His eyes narrowed. "I don't need your trust."

I tipped my head back and laughed. "You do if you want to put a child in my belly." I grabbed my womb and his eyes flared like the sun, a slight pink going to his cheeks.

He cleared his throat and a small part of me felt triumph for making him blush.

"How long have you known you can transform into a dragon?" he asked, ignoring everything I'd said.

I rolled my eyes. "Last night was the first time."

His eyes narrowed as if trying to sense a lie.

"Truth," I said smugly.

That made his nostrils flare.

"Are you an assassin here to kill me?" he asked, and I couldn't help but laugh. The look on his face wiped the smile from mine.

"No," I told him honestly.

He frowned, as if frustrated I was telling the truth.

"Is the woman who raised you your real mother?" he suddenly said, and my heart stopped beating for a moment.

He'd gone right for the kill and my lips turned into a frown. My *real* mother. What the Hades did that mean? I knew what he meant, but to me she *was* my real mother. I knew I couldn't lie to him anymore or he would kill me, but out of respect for my mother I would speak my truth.

"Yes, she will always be my *real* mother, but... she did not give birth to me." I tipped my chin high, cursing the stupid tear that rolled down my cheek.

He looked conflicted, no doubt weighing my answer. "How long have you known?"

"She just told me the day you came to take Kendal and I away," I said flatly.

His face softened with each truth I divulged and I realized then that I *did* need to earn his trust. What life would I have if my own king didn't trust me?

"Did she tell you what you are?" he asked, and there was a hint of compassion in his voice.

What did that mean?

"What am I?" I asked, suddenly scared of what that answer would be.

His stern look was back. "What did your mother tell you on the day that I came to get you?"

I chewed the inside of my lip. My mother said not to trust him, but my cover was blown so now it was Plan B: make him fall in love with me, which was going *amazingly*.

Not.

I was on to Plan C, which was: *Don't get killed.*

I released the air I was holding. "First, tell me something to help me trust you. I can't smell a lie, but I do wonder why you are so desperate for an heir when you just barely lost your beloved wife."

His face took on a pained expression and he rubbed the side of his jaw, assessing me. "My magic is linked to the dragon-folk people," he said, and I nodded. This was well known. "With each passing day that I do not produce an heir to strengthen and double the magic, our people get weaker, and *I* get weaker."

I gasped.

"Pretty soon, I won't be able to transform at all, and the people connected to me will lose their magic."

His truth hit me like a ton of bricks. Dragon-folk without their magic *died*. There was a well-known story about one dragon-folk woman who had her magic sucked away by the fae king, and instead of just becoming human, she shriveled into a husk of death. We were nothing without our magic... it kept our entire human form alive. Even as a hybrid one could not just live with their human half.

"I..." I didn't know what to say.

"Your turn." He assessed me with those cool green eyes and I nodded. He'd shared something with me, something very personal, now it was my turn.

"The woman who gave birth to me was passing

through town. My mother said she arrived heavily pregnant, a highborn, covered in blood, and spoke of a battle where her entire family was slaughtered for a magic they held."

He frowned. "Eighteen winters ago? There were no Eclipse Dragons left then, unless..." Something dawned on his face and he fell against the wall, his back hitting it hard. "My grandfather died eighteen winters ago. Fighting a threat to the crown, my father said."

A silence descended over the both of us. Was he saying that his grandfather killed my birth mother's entire family and made her go into early labor with me?

So Narine's story was true? The Eclipse Dragons? The Lost Royal?

I cleared my throat. "The woman told my mother that her family was murdered for the magic they held, and that if anyone ever detected this magic in her child... in me, that I would be killed. Then she died of blood loss."

He inhaled my truth, then let out a long suffering sigh, watching me closely.

"She was right. I *should* kill you."

I wasn't prepared for his words, for *his* truth, and it caused a ripple of shock to run up my body.

I gasped. "Why? I've done nothing wrong to you!" My gaze flicked to the exit as I dreamed of escaping, but there was no way I could get past him, and if I did, Regina would be waiting for me just outside the door.

He shook his head. "You truly don't know what you are? What your magic can do to me? To any dragon-folk?"

"Obviously not! I just found out I had wings yesterday. And then I was thrown in jail! I've had no time to run to the library and research!"

He shot me a glare that warned me that my attitude was not welcome.

This man is infuriating!

He stepped closer and then leaned forward, placing his hands on either side of my chair so that his face was inches from mine. Being this close to him robbed me of oxygen and filled my body with a pulsing heat I wasn't prepared for. My mind went fuzzy, and as I stared into his ember gaze I wondered if he was going to kiss me.

"Arwen Novakson, you are the lost queen of the Eclipse Dragon clan, and your magic is so powerful that it can devour mine, killing me and *all* of the dragon-folk people that are connected to me. You, Arwen, are the king killer."

I went stock still, not even daring to breathe. Pain,

shame and fear rushed through my system in equal measure. Unshed tears filled my eyes, blurring my vision. *Narine was right.*

"No," I finally managed, and he pushed off the chair and started to pace the room.

"Yes. Your kin made an agreement with the Nightfall queen centuries ago to kill my father and drain our people of magic, fulfilling the Nightfall queen's dream of a human utopia devoid of magic."

"No," I argued, though I didn't even know anything about my kin to know if it was true or not.

"Yes," he growled, black curls of smoke coming out his nose. "We have detailed records. Spies that my great-great grandfather sent who witnessed meetings between the Nightfall queen and the Eclipse Dragon queen."

My heart hammered in my chest at his words. "So your great-great grandfather killed the Eclipse clan queen?"

"Kill or be killed." He crossed his arms and stared me down.

"But the people tied to her..."

"Eclipse Dragon magic is not tied to a people like mine is. Their queens do not need heirs for power. They are unique in that way." He sounded absolutely pissed off about that.

I frowned. "Then where are the Eclipse Dragon folk today, the ones with blue magic like me? If not tied to her, they wouldn't have died with her."

He sighed. "The Eclipse clan queen killed nearly all of them. She wanted her family to be the last dragons left in the realm. She absorbed their power, making herself virtually immortal."

Immortal.

A person with at least a quarter dragon-folk magic lived about a hundred years, a full-blooded royal about a hundred and fifty. If she consumed magic from hundreds of dragon-folk... I shook my head, trying to process it all.

"But the Eclipse clan people... she killed them? Wouldn't it be in our history books?"

A realization hit me.

"The Plague... it wasn't a plague, was it?" I thought of the stories of people shriveling up and dying, being found in their tents dry as a husk. It was about two centuries ago... probably right when all of this happened.

He shook his head. "It wasn't a plague. That was a cover story to keep the people from panicking. The king killer can take magic from any dragon-folk, absorbing it and leaving them to ashes, making *herself* more powerful."

I jumped to my feet, startling him.

"All of those children," I sobbed, suddenly feeling sick, remembering the stories of the little children who died in the "plague."

"The queen of the Eclipse Dragons killed them. They all died." His tone was resolute.

An immense sadness smacked into me, taking my breath away and causing my knees to go weak. I fell to the ground as a sob ripped from my throat.

I couldn't stop thinking of the little children that the plague took... but it wasn't a plague. It was my great-great grandmother. I didn't have anything to do with that genocide, and yet it stained my soul, seeped into the very core of my being, and I accepted that I had a role in it even if just by birthright.

Anger rushed through my veins. I had more questions than answers, and everyone in my line was dead, so I would never get those answers. I was so mad my skin felt hot.

"Your nose is smoking," he told me.

I looked down. A small tendril of white smoke drifted to the ceiling. A shriek escaped my throat and I stumbled backwards, hoping to get away from it.

"Calm down." The king held out his hands. "Your dragon fire might come out."

I pinned him with a glare. "I can't help it."

He ignored me. "Take a deep breath and calm down."

Stupid male! I hated nothing more than being told to calm down when I was mad. The smoke was thicker now and I was fully freaking out.

Would I really breathe fire? If I did, it might burn the king, and then he *would* really have reason to kill me.

I closed my eyes and inhaled slowly; the char of smoke splashed across my tongue for a second and then I breathed out.

My eyes opened and he was inches from my face.

"I'm calm. No need to kill me," I said with as much sarcasm as I could manage.

"I'll decide that." His tone held more seriousness than I would have liked.

I could feel the blood flee from my face. "My king, I would *never* drain your power and kill your people."

There was surprise in his eyes. Maybe it was because I'd called him my king, or maybe it was because he'd heard the truth in my statement.

"If I kill you, I kill my very own sister. Use your head, you idiot!" I snapped, irritated with him.

"I *am* an idiot. I'm an idiot for liking you!" he yelled back at me, and then looked up at me with a vulnerability I wasn't prepared for.

His jaw clamped down, but I didn't regret calling him an idiot. I'd been truthful with him this whole time and he knew it. He stepped closer to me, not backing away, and my body wanted to inch closer to his. Even now, knowing that he decided my fate, I wanted to feel his arms around me.

"I liked you back, dammit!" I screamed, and then before I knew what was happening I rushed forward and pressed my lips to his mouth.

His inhale of surprise sucked my breath into his mouth and made me second-guess what the Hades I was doing. Before I could retreat and chide myself for making a move on him, his hands came around my waist and crushed me flat against his body. I swiped my tongue across his and an angry moan ripped from his throat as he consumed me. Being this close to him, pressed against him, actually made something deep inside of me ache. I ached to be even closer, I ached to be one with him. His tongue swiped across mine again and a shock of energy passed between us. Much like that day in the kissing tent.

It was him.

I pulled backwards in surprise, my hands flung to my mouth.

The king's chest heaved as he stared at me with glowing yellow eyes as he no doubt wrestled with my fate. Did I imagine the small shock just now? Did I imagine that this kiss was so similar to the one in the kissing tent? *It couldn't have been him?* He'd been outside the walls waiting, right? My mind spun with this new revelation.

After what seemed like forever he sighed, looking tired. "I've found you innocent of treason and will allow you to roam the castle freely, but do not leave Jade City until I can find out what I'm going to do with you. Okay?"

I sagged in relief at the announcement that my impending death had been canceled. I hoped he didn't think that my kissing him was to try to change that, but after I had walked in here with an unbuttoned tunic, I feared that was exactly what he did think. I guessed we were just going to ignore the fact that the kiss had ever happened.

Fine by me. I was way too freaked out about it being just like the kissing tent kiss to even fathom it.

"Wait, what do you mean *'What you're going to do with me?'*" He wasn't still thinking of killing me, was he?

He squeezed the bridge of his nose. "Good day, Arwen." He dismissed me.

I huffed, but before I could retort, Regina opened the door. "Let me escort you to your room, my lady."

Did he call her in?

As I passed him, I looked over at him, hoping to convey how I was feeling with a look. But I wasn't sure how I was feeling. I wanted to kiss him again. But then also smack him for being an idiot and jailing me and interrogating me. Whatever he saw on my face couldn't have been good, because his jaw clenched.

Oops.

Regina and I walked in silence back to the room, and when I reached the door she faced me. "I told you he was a just king."

She'd been right. I had expected him to half torture and then kill me, and all we'd done was yell at each other for half an hour and then kiss.

"Thank you," I murmured. I couldn't believe I'd spent the last few days with my idol and she'd seen all of these embarrassing things.

"Good day, my lady." She curtsied and then left me at the door to my quarters.

When I stepped into the room, Narine was waiting, wringing her fingers together anxiously.

"You're alive!" she exclaimed.

I nodded. "I'm free to roam but not leave the city," I told her.

My gaze fell to the damp emerald-green dress on the floor by her feet, and the bowl of dirty water with a scrub brush that lay beside it. It was horribly stained with dirt and splotches that weren't coming out.

"I'm so sorry."

She waved me off. "I'll figure it out. I'm just glad you're okay."

That was a nice thing to say but it was total crap. "How? How will you figure it out?"

This dress wouldn't sell, and no more dresses would be coming in. She wouldn't be able to pay for her sister's wedding.

She chewed the inside of her lip, almost brought to tears. "I'll manage, alright? Do you mind if I leave you early today so that I can talk to the buyer and figure this out?"

She gestured to the dress.

I nodded, guilt washing over me. "Of course."

With a shy smile, she scooped the beautiful emerald-green dress up into her arms and left the apartment.

Leaving me alone to my tumultuous thoughts was a *bad* idea. My mind chewed on a hundred different things. Narine's sister's wedding wouldn't happen because I ruined the dress. The king was possibly still thinking about killing me. Kendal was sent home. Joslyn and some of the other girls were still here competing for the king's hand, a hand in marriage that

I would be lying if I said I didn't now want. That kiss—oh Maker that kiss—had confused the Hades out of me! And I was some lost queen? It was too much.

I needed to go for a walk.

Leaving my room, I exited the dormitory wing and headed in search of the library. Maybe I could find something about the Lost Royal or Eclipse Dragons there. I was sure it was this way, just beyond the kitchen, but when I reached it I realized it was a dead end. I turned, remembering that the library was in fact in the opposite direction.

I passed a room with the door cracked open. King Valdren's voice filtered out into the hallway.

"Which one of them has the best chance of giving me a healthy child?" he asked someone.

"Technically, Arwen has the most magic." It was Dr. Elsie who answered, and upon hearing my own name, I froze. "But we have no idea what an Eclipse royal and a Dark Night royal would breed. The magic created could be... incredibly powerful *or* catastrophic."

No one said anything for a full minute, and I should have walked away... but I couldn't. I wanted to hear his response. This involved me after all.

"Joslyn is your *safest* choice, my lord," Dr. Elsie said.

"But Arwen is a choice I could also make?" The hope in the king's tone made butterflies flutter in my stomach.

"I'm afraid I have to advise against that, my lord," a male voice said. I recognized it as the old man with the leather-bound tome from the testing room. He must be a top advisor.

"She is a king killer. A queen of the Eclipse Dragons. She carries the power to completely annihilate you and your entire clan. You must never forget that."

"I haven't," the king growled. "But I have interrogated her and she is blameless. She had no idea of her heritage."

He stuck up for me! My body was glued to the wall in anticipation of how the conversation would end.

"And yet now that she knows the power she wields, the lands she could lay claim to, what will she do with that information?"

Lands to lay claim to? Did they think I wanted a palace and throne at Cinder Mountain? That was ridiculous.

"It is my advice that you take her out before she does the same to you," the man said, and I froze in fear.

"Master Augustson!" Dr. Elsie scolded.

King Valdren's voice was so gritty it could cut glass: "Is that what you advised my grandfather eighteen winters ago? Advice that got him killed and thrust my father into power?"

I wished to peer into the room and see the look on everyone's faces. I wanted to know for certain if that was how my birth mother's family died? If Drae's grandfather killed them, causing my mother to flee to Cinder Village and gave birth to me.

"Joslyn is a fine choice, my lord," the man concluded, not answering the question.

"I agree. She has more magic than Queen Amelia did. Not much, but slightly more," Dr. Elsie said.

Silence. The longest stretch of silence I'd ever had to endure.

"Alright, if that is your assessment, I agree. Tell Joslyn I've chosen her and start tracking her monthly cycles. We can be married in a moon's time. I'll deal with Arwen." His words simultaneously broke my heart and sent a chill down my spine.

I moved quickly out of the hallway and back toward my rooms.

He's going to marry Joslyn.

The safe bet.

I should be happy for her, for him, for my sister and all of the dragon-folk who would be saved by the heir they would create, but I was also angry. He didn't love Joslyn. He wanted a child and was just marrying her out of duty in order to protect her purity and image. I guess she should be grateful he wasn't just taking her as some mistress whore. For some reason, hearing them speak of Joslyn and I in terms of magical rank really rubbed me wrong.

But could I blame him? His people, all of the dragon-folk, depended on him to have an heir. Would I do the same in his position? *Probably*. But for a moment it had sounded like he'd wanted to pick me, and that had made me excited. Sure we screamed at each other, and he'd imprisoned me, but... there was something there with him. A deep connection I couldn't explain, something I never experienced before.

Forgetting my earlier desire to go to the library, I went into my room and curled under the covers of my bed instead. Any minute now someone was going to come tell me I was going home or going to be hung, I was sure of it.

Now I knew what the king had meant when he'd said he'd deal with me. He was thinking on whether he should marry me for my magical dragon womb or kill me because I had the power to kill him.

I'll deal with Arwen. His words haunted me. What did that mean? He wouldn't really take the advice of that man, would he?

I threw the covers off of my head and burst to my feet.

He was going to kill me. He was *totally* going to kill me. Just one more dragon to take out like his grandfather had, and then he'd have no more problems.

I raced across the room, searching the drawers for my hunter's outfit that my mother and Kendal had made me. I found it in the bottom drawer of the dresser scrubbed mostly clean, with my hunting blade on top.

Thank you, *Narine*.

I grabbed it, shoving it into an empty shoulder bag, and then tucked the knife into my waistband. Running to the small kitchen off my living room, I threw some dried fruits and cheeses into the bag as well, and filled my canteen. Maybe if I could steal a horse I could make it out of the main gates before they realized I was gone and sounded the alarm.

Slipping out of the door to my living quarters, I hurried down the hall, trying not to look like a fugitive fleeing.

When I passed Annabeth, the lead housemaid, I gave her a wave. "Good day for a stroll," I said.

She smiled and nodded. "The gardens are beautiful this time of year."

Yep, going to the gardens, nothing suspicious about me. When I reached the end of the hallway that led to the outside, I pushed the doors wide and broke into a run.

I was a bit discombobulated at first. I'd only been out here a few times and it took me a moment to get my bearings. The stables and horse barns were to the right, so I aimed that way just before I heard a shout behind me.

"Arwen, stop!" the king commanded.

Pure terror ripped through me as I ran past a stable maid and then veered to the left, spotting a labyrinth of high hedges I could get lost in. I sprinted across the yard and burst into the protection of the tall hedge, but the sound of the footsteps behind me was too close.

Reaching behind me, I grasped for my hunting knife just as a body slammed into me. I tripped over my own feet, spinning in midair as King Valdren's arms came around my shoulders. My butt hit the ground first, and then my back, and finally the thud of my skull. Luckily, it was soft grass, but that did not save me from the giant man who landed on top of me, making a whoosh of air leave me in a rush.

His thighs pinned my hips to the spot, and I hated the heat that crept up my body at his touch.

"Were you about to pull a knife on me?" He looked down at me incredulously, his eyes wild and dark hair strewn about.

Our bodies were smashed together, pressed fully against each other, and I could feel my cheeks redden from the close contact. I'd never been like this with a man...

He seemed to pick up on my dumbfounded loss of speech, and rolled off of me, taking my hunting knife with him.

With the absence of his body, I could breathe and think. "I will defend my life if attacked, yes," I told him, and sat up, looking up at his giant form, which now blotted out the sun.

He reached out a hand to me and I raised one eyebrow, staring at him skeptically.

"I won't bite," he said, and I took the offered hand, allowing him to pull me up.

When I was finally facing him, or more accurately craning my neck to look up at him, I steeled myself.

"I am marrying Joslyn."

I didn't expect the pang of hurt to slice into my chest, especially because I'd just heard him tell his advisors that.

I nodded. "Congratulations."

Why did I sound bitter?

"My advisors say that I cannot allow you to go home, where you could plot to take over my kingdom—"

I barked out in laughter at such a preposterous thing, but his glare shut me up.

"So you have to kill me." I eyed the hunting blade in his hand. Would he kill me with my own blade? Right here in the privacy of the labyrinth hedge? Panic invaded my entire body.

I'm too young to die.

He looked hurt at my accusation, peering deeply into my eyes. "I could never kill you, Arwen." He sounded upset at that declaration, and somehow those words sounded romantic coming from him. I relaxed a little and he stepped closer.

"I came to ask you if you wanted to join my Royal Guard," he said. "You seemed excited about the prospect the day that I mentioned it, and so... there is a spot for you, if you want."

My mouth popped open in shock. I tried to speak but couldn't find the words. Was he ill? He found out I was able to siphon his power and kill everyone and now he wanted me as one of his protectors?

He gazed at me expectantly, as if waiting for an answer. He was serious. Laughter bubbled up inside of me and a lightness pulled at my limbs. "Be a member of the Royal Guard, are you kidding? That's my dream!"

I got taken with the moment and threw myself into his arms, hugging him. His body stiffened and I pulled back, reprimanding myself for how inappropriate that was.

"Sorry. I got excited." I stepped away from him, painfully aware that I had no highborn manners and had probably broken a million rules with this man. This *king*.

He nodded. "You have little fear of danger, which is what I look for in a Royal Guardsman-woman. The way you behaved that day with the attack on Gypsy Rock was admirable. I'll train you to control your dragon powers, and Regina will train you in combat. I think you will be a great asset to my kingdom."

I did a curtsy, bowing my head as well for good measure. "I accept your gracious offer."

He frowned, looking a bit disturbed with my eagerness. "You do realize that you are a queen by birthright and I will be relegating you to *my* service for the rest of your life?"

I nodded eagerly. "I'm no queen. I'm just a hunter who wants to take care of my family. I'll follow you wherever you lead, Your Highness."

His face went slack, his breathing slowing. Something I said had struck a chord with him. I didn't say anything bad, so I wasn't sure if I should apologize or not. He looked deeply into my eyes and it felt like the air had magnetized around us. It was thick with something tangible. I had the strongest urge to reach out and touch him, to stroke his neck like I'd stroked his dragon that day.

That brought my thoughts back to our kiss. Had it also been him in the May Day tent? That was crazy, right?

His gaze fell to my lips as if he too were thinking about the kiss, and I swallowed hard. "Can I have my knife back?" I asked, reaching out and hoping to break whatever spell had been thrown over me that was causing me to want to touch him constantly.

He cleared his throat and handed it to me, but not before he looked my body up and down. "It's a fine hunting knife, but you'll need a proper sword soon. A bow and arrow too."

The joy of getting new weapons must have been evident on my face, because the corners of his lips turned up slightly.

"I hope this new arrangement suits the both of us. Good day, Arwen." He tipped his head.

"Good day, my lord," I said, feeling giddy with the prospect of joining the Royal Guard.

"You may call me Drae," he said, and then walked away.

First name basis with the king? This couldn't have

gone better. Not only was he not going to kill me, I was going to be joining his Royal Guard!

Narine's sister's wedding floated into my mind then and I called after him. "Wait!"

He stopped, looking over his shoulder at me.

"Is there a salary for the position in your army?"

He appraised me. "Of course. One hundred jade coins per moon."

That was exactly how much Narine needed!

"But I'll be able to stay in the castle and eat for free?" I questioned.

He nodded. "You will."

"Can I possibly have an advance on my first moon's payment? There is something really important I need to buy. It cannot delay." I swallowed hard. Asking a man for money never felt good. Asking the king for an advance on a job I hadn't started felt awful. But I wanted to surprise Narine with the payment for her sister's wedding in full.

His brows drew together. "Do you have a gambling problem I don't know about?"

I laughed. "No, and in the spirit of no more lying... it's for my maid's little sister's wedding."

He stared at me for a moment, maybe reading into my answers, and then his brows drew together to form a knot in his head. "You would pay an entire month's salary to a maid you've known less than a moon?"

I nodded, hoping he wouldn't say no or tell Annabeth.

"Very well. See the castle merchant tomorrow," he said. "I will clear it."

When he finally left, I couldn't believe how much my luck had changed. I'd be able to send most of the money home every month to my mother and sister, and I'd have the job of my dreams. The king would get his heir with Joslyn and everything was going to work out...

Then why did it feel like someone had carved a hole in my chest with a knife?

"What's this?" Narine asked, wide-eyed as I tossed the pouch of one hundred jade coins into her open palm. I'd gone first thing this morning to the castle merchant and he'd had a bag of coins all ready for me.

"That is your sister's wedding payment, and you have the rest of the day off to go deal with your affairs," I told her, unable to keep the grin off my face.

"How!?" she shrieked, laughing as she opened the

bag to peer inside. Tears rolled down her cheeks and she looked up at me.

"I got a job. That's my first moon's advance," I stated.

She shook her head, trying to hand me back the bag. "No, I can't. It's too generous. You have your own sister's wedding to pay for one day."

I chuckled. "Weddings in Cinder Village cost ten jade coins, and everyone brings a dish of food to share. Trust me, I can afford this."

She chewed at her lip, shaking her head in amazement. "I... I don't know what to say. What job did you get? Here in Jade City?"

"I've been asked to join the king's Royal Guard. I start my first practice in an hour, after I pledge loyalty to the king."

Narine's brown eyebrows hit her hairline. "The king asked you to join his Royal Guard after all that?"

"I know. Crazy, right?"

She nodded. "I'll say. Did you hear the news that he's marrying Joslyn?"

I inclined my head, trying to keep the emotion out of my face.

"I heard he's desperate for an heir but no one knows why. He grieved over Queen Amelia so hard, no one thought he would remarry so soon, but..." her voice trailed off.

I knew why. But it was my secret with King Valdren. *Drae*, now that we were on a first-name basis. I respected him enough to keep it private. If people knew that their magic and very livelihood was tied up in him having an heir, it would create a panic across the realm.

"He must have been really taken with Joslyn," I said.

Narine nodded, and wished me a good day before leaving with her coins.

I left my quarters and made my way outside to the training grounds with pep in my step. I was wearing my mother's leather armor and I was ready to be a Royal Guard badass like Regina.

I made my way quickly to the great hall, where Regina had asked me to meet her and the king for my loyalty swearing. When I got there, she was waiting outside the door with her hands clasped behind her back.

"Ready?" she asked.

I nodded. I had no idea what this little adventure would involve, but I was prepared to pledge my allegiance to the king and be knighted or whatever into his army.

She opened the large double doors and I glanced up, my breath catching in my throat. Nearly the *entire* army was here. And it looked like some highborn families too. The Royal Guard stood in perfect rows, facing the aisle that I was now walking up with Regina beside me. I wanted to shrink into myself and die. I hadn't expected this kind of a crowd. It seemed like a way bigger deal than I had expected. When we reached the front, I gave polite smiles to the highborn families, confused as to why everyone was here for a simple oath of loyalty.

When I reached the raised dais, I looked up at the king, who sat in his high-backed throne. The throne was made of black metal to mimic dragon scales; the design resembled flames that grew up the back and fanned out behind him. He watched me with yellow eyes as I approached him.

Regina bowed her head as we stood before him, so I did the same, my heart hammering in my throat.

What if he lied? What if he was never going to let me be in his guard and he was about to cut my head off?

There was a scraping of metal as he stood up from the throne and approached me. "Much of our history has been hidden by our forefathers, but many of you know that there were once *two* dragon clans," the king's voice bellowed, echoing throughout the hall. "When testing Lady Arwen for magic, we discovered she is a lost member of the Eclipse Dragon clan."

Gasps and murmurs rang out behind me and I froze, unprepared for his revelation. I hadn't thought he was going to tell people about me... I suddenly felt naked with my secret displayed for all to hear, but also realized he hadn't called me a lost *queen*, he was keeping that to himself.

"She will be a great asset to my army, and I am honored to have her public pledge of loyalty," he declared.

This felt like a *big* deal, like a way bigger deal than I had prepared myself for. I was totally going to faint.

"Kneel," Regina told me in a soft whisper.

I dropped to both knees, head still bowed, and the king descended four steps to the bottom level and approached me.

"Face your king," Regina said, and I looked up into King Valdren's endless green eyes. I couldn't decide which color I liked best, the green or yellow. He was changing them so often with his emotions, I wondered if he even noticed.

"Lady Arwen Novakson of Cinder Mountain." *Lady* was a highborn designation. By calling me that, he was telling everyone I had highborn status with a single word.

"Yes, my king?" I gazed into his eyes as he watched me closely. When he looked at me, it was as if he was reading me like a book.

"Do you swear loyalty to me as your king and ruler, for as long as you shall live? To protect me and my family over your very own life?"

"I do," I said, projecting my voice for all to hear.

The crowd erupted into applause. I went to stand, then the king held out his hands, indicating everyone to quiet.

I stayed where I was.

"And do you swear to never harm me with your magic?" he added.

Hurt rose up inside of me as my throat tightened with emotion. I could tell from the look on Regina's face that he didn't ask everyone that, and the fact that he *still* didn't fully trust me stung like salt on a wound.

"I do, my king," I all but growled.

His face relaxed, and the crowd again broke into applause, but I stayed where I kneeled.

"May I rise now? Or would you like to ask me anything else?" I said to him. The people gathered were clapping so loudly that only Regina and the king probably heard me.

He gave me a smirk. "You may rise, my lady."

I stood, brushing off my knees. Reaching into his pocket, he pulled out a breast plate fitted with the Royal Guard insignia. The background was black with a gold dragon emblem. The only thing missing was the red that designated a Drayken elite guard, but I planned to move my way up through the ranks over the years and get that too.

"Welcome to the Royal Guard, Arwen." He handed me the plate, and I couldn't help the foolish grin that graced my face.

"Good luck with practice," he told me, and then turned and left the room.

Okay, that was a slightly weird and overdone event for a mere five minutes. The people present didn't seem to mind that the king had left them, because they all continued to chat among themselves, and the Royal Guard rushed forward to congratulate me.

I smiled and thanked them. Regina leaned into my shoulder to whisper in my ear: "I know you haven't had an easy time here, and I'm about to become your commanding officer, so I can't show special treatment." I nodded and her lips peeled back into a huge smile. "But as a woman, I have to say, I'm damned proud to have you in the guard. It's a pleasure, Arwen."

My heart felt light and fluttery. I'd been obsessed

with stories of Regina Wayfeather since I was a wee babe. I would pass the tavern and hear the men talk about her and all of the amazing battles she fought in.

"The pleasure is mine, Regina."

Her face then fell into a cool mask of calm. "You can call me Commander now."

"Yes, Commander." I guess that thirty seconds of bonding was all we were going to get. She looked like she was about to put me through Hades.

"Calston!" Regina called someone away from a group of other warriors that he'd been talking to.

A tall man a few winters older than me with broad shoulders and sandy-blond hair approached us. He wore his hair in the same style as the king, the sides shaved and a long braid down the back. The designation of a warrior of high ranking.

He stood at stiff attention before Regina. "Yes, Commander?"

"Can you show Lady Arwen to the armory, and then bring her to the pup training field? I need to get down there."

Pup training field? That was what they called us?

He nodded to her and she left.

He then turned and faced me. "Lady Arwen." He bowed.

It was weird to be bowed to and to be called a lady,

but I guessed it was protocol now that the king had outed me as a highborn.

"Er, Calston?" I curtsied and he grinned, causing me to be taken aback by his handsomeness. There was a deep dimple in his right cheek.

"You don't curtsy to me, I'm not a highborn," he told me. "And now that you are in the king's Royal Guard, you only have to bow your head to him briefly."

I swallowed hard, my cheeks reddening. "Noted. I'm not really a highborn either. I mean, I guess by blood, but I grew up in Cinder Village."

He smiled easily at me, flashing bright white straight teeth. "I'm from a tiny village outside Grim Hollow, and my friends call me Cal."

"Cal." I nodded.

He reached out and touched the small of my back, leading me away from the busy crowd and to a side door. After opening the door for me and waiting until I walked through it first, he met me in the silent hallway.

"Be honest," he asked me as we walked down the corridor and past the library. "How awkward was that for you back there at the ceremony in front of everyone?"

I laughed, instantly liking his realness. "So awkward. Regina didn't warn me that there would be that many people."

"She likes to see the new pups squirm."

"How long will I be called a pup?" I grumbled.

He chuckled. "Until you've seen your first battle."

I puffed my chest up. "I've killed a Nightfall warrior while riding on the dragon king's back."

He gave me a side look that indicated he was impressed.

"I heard. Wait until you've killed a dozen of the enemy in the span of a few minutes. Then we will no longer call you a pup."

A dozen? The thought made me sick, but I was a member of the Royal Guard now so I'd have to get used to it.

Kill or be killed.

I nodded and he opened a door at the end of the hall, stepping outside. We crossed the courtyard to another building and then stood before two giant iron doors.

"Thad!" Cal pounded on the door and it opened, revealing a short man with a giant belly who was holding five wooden swords.

"Training swords?" Thad asked.

Cal nodded, plucking one of them off of the pile and handing it to me, then taking the others to bring them to the training field.

It was heavier than I expected but not as heavy as

the king's blade. I didn't want a little weak training sword, especially not after the king said I needed a proper sword and bow and arrow, but I kept my mouth shut.

"Have there even been any other women in the Royal Guard?" I asked as we walked across the green rolling lawn.

Cal gave me a serious look. "No, lady. Just you and Regina."

I hoped that wouldn't be a thing... I wanted to be accepted like any of the rest of them. I was a good hunter, and I was sure I'd make a great fighter given some proper training.

"You must have great power for the king to have asked you into the Royal Guard," Cal said, and I suddenly grew quiet, holding the sword awkwardly as we continued our trek.

"I guess," I mumbled.

Cal stopped and faced me, which caused me to stop as well and meet his blue eyes. "The king doesn't allow women in the Royal Guard unless they are so powerful he fears not having them close."

I swallowed hard, because it sounded like a warning. "Is Regina powerful, then?" I tried to steer the conversation away from me.

He chuckled. "She's got the most power out of all

of us. She could burn a tall building with one breath if she desired."

She could breathe fire that large? That was incredible.

"So Eclipse clan?" he asked, looking down at me incredulously. "I thought... I mean, how is that possible?"

I did *not* want to talk about that. He was sweet and he meant well, but I had to be careful here. "I have no idea." I shrugged, spotting Regina off in the distance. I waved to her, even though she wasn't looking at me. "Coming!" I shouted, and took off at a brisk walk.

The king had outed my Eclipse clan lineage because the men might eventually see my blue fire and wings, but they didn't need to know any more than that.

When I made it to the training field, Regina was barking orders at a few men who stood before her.

Walking up to her, I waved giddily. "Hey, we got the training—"

"You're late, and you're moons behind this new rookie squadron," she barked at me. "Take your sword and pick a partner. You'll need three practices a day to get in fighting shape. Weak soldiers get killed, and I won't have that on my watch."

I gulped. All pretenses of this being a morning

bonding with my new squadron were dashed. She wasn't kidding about not showing me any special treatment.

"Yes, Commander." I hefted my sword and stood next to some scrawny guy who looked lost.

"Up," Regina cried, and held her sword before her, straight up to the sky. "Cross right," she barked, and brought it down and to the right. The other men did as she did, so I quickly got into line and mimicked the motions.

"Cross left." She brought the sword to the left.

"And down." She slashed the sword down.

Then we did that five thousand more times. Maybe not that many, but it felt like it. My arms felt like the bones had melted and all that was left was skin and blood. As Regina called an end to practice, they quivered as I tried to hold the sword up.

"Get some food," Regina called out to the group, but then tipped her head to me, indicating I stay behind.

I walked over to her side and she looked from me to Cal. "Come back after lunch and work with Cal. You'll need to catch up."

Cal had been assisting Regina for the entire class and had now apparently been made my tutor. He gave me a smile, and again I was struck by how handsome he was. Maybe not marrying the king, being independent with my own job and salary, was going to be the biggest blessing of all.

Maybe if I told myself that enough times I might even believe it was true.

Three Weeks Later.

I'd heard that Hades was a horrible fate for any soul, full of constant torment and pain in the afterlife. Well, I'd gotten a taste of it over the past three weeks under Regina and Cal's constant "care." It was like they were trying to bring me to the brink of death each and every day, and only when I was ready to meet the Maker did they allow me to go home and rest. My leather hunting suit no longer fit.

I'd bulked up in every area due to the constant hefting of heavy weapons and eating of rich foods. The palace seamstress was going to take it out for me and add a side panel today.

Despite the constant practices, bruises, and even stitches, I'd never been stronger, faster, or more lethal. I'd learned to wield a sword in combat and spit fire on my enemy. I even learned that I had self-healing powers. A wound that would have taken me weeks to heal before was now gone within a day.

I had three practices a day, one with Regina and my pup squadron, one with Cal, and the other with the king himself. The king and my practices were secret, where he taught me to use my dragon magic.

Joslyn and the king were officially engaged to be married in a week's time. Sometimes she came to the practices, which was a little awkward. I'd gotten a front seat as I watched her fall in love with the king, but it was clear he did not share her affections. He was respectful to her, cared for her needs, but he did not hold her hand, didn't kiss her, and she'd confided in me that she feared it was going to be a marriage of convenience.

I had also grown close to her, considered her one of my good friends. She was kind, strong, and thoughtful, and we spent nearly every evening taking a walk around the gardens and talking about our day. It was good to have someone else who knew about your situation, and both Joslyn's and my situations were unique. She was going to be the future queen of Embergate, and she'd been let in on the secret that I was the Lost Royal. The king killer. All those titles I shunned. I'd rather be known as a good hunter or even a pup in the Royal Guard.

I stood in the training field waiting on the king as I bit into an apple. Joslyn was sunning on a nearby rock with her dark hair splayed out behind her.

"Your mom and sister are coming for the Fall Moon Festival, right?" Joslyn asked.

I nodded, unable to keep the grin off my face. I hadn't seen them since I came here nearly a moon ago, but I'd sent home a letter with a royal courier telling them of my new job, and my mother seemed happy with my new position in the Royal Guard. "Drae said that she and my sister could stay in the palace."

The king and I were on a first-name basis, and I hated to admit it but I considered him one of my closest friends. We saw each other every day for practice, and he was so patient in teaching me new things and so easy to talk to. Ever since I joined the Royal Guard and took that pledge before everyone, it was like he fully trusted me. Gone was the stuffy king with an unreadable gaze. Now, he was just... Drae.

"What a nice king he is to have done that." Drae's voice came from behind me and Joslyn burst into laughter as I rolled my eyes.

"He's okay at times," I admitted, causing him to lightly shove me in the shoulder.

"Hello, Drae," Joslyn said awkwardly, sitting up and waving too eagerly at him.

"How are you today?" he asked her kindly.

She gave him a small smile. "Good. I got a new dress made." She spread her hands over the bright yellow silk and looked up at him expectantly.

It was clear she was fishing for a compliment.

Drae sighed, reading into her need for attention. He sidestepped me and faced her, leaning down to kiss her cheek. "You look beautiful," he said.

She did look beautiful; it wasn't a lie.

Joslyn placed her hands over his, beaming up at him, probably desperate for his touch, and a small ache formed in my chest as I watched Drae hover over her while she gazed up at him with adoration.

I wanted that. I wanted someone to touch and hold and... kiss.

I hadn't kissed anyone since that day in the interrogation room with Drae, and now that I knew he was marrying Joslyn I wanted to move on. My sword trainer, Cal, and I had become close, and there had been multiple near misses where I thought he meant to kiss me, but something was holding him back. I decided that today I was going to ask him about it.

After my training with the king.

Drae pulled away from Joslyn and faced me. "You can spit fire in a stream of forty feet, throw fireballs from your hands five at a time. I think it's time we mastered flight."

Anxiety churned in my gut and Joslyn stood abruptly.

"My king, last time she—"

He cut Joslyn off. "If she is to fight beside me in battle, I must know she is a capable flier."

Sick unease washed over me. I'd transformed a grand total of three times.

Once at my magic test. The second time in practice with Drae and Regina, and that time my arms and legs had transformed too. The third time was last week, when my entire body had transformed into a blue dragon and Drae had convinced me to go flying with him. It had been windy outside, so my wing caught the air wrong, buckled, and I fell in a dead fifty-foot drop. Although my dragon magic afforded me advanced healing, it took two days for me to walk again without pain, and I was not keen to relive that.

"I... I'm scared to. I can't," I admitted.

He shook his head. "You can and you will. If you let the fear take hold, you will never fly, and what use is a dragon who cannot fly?"

I groaned, looking up at the sky for any hint of wind.

There was none.

The Nightfall queen was constantly threatening our bridges at the Great River. They said it was only a matter of time before she broke through our defenses there again. She wanted the king and all the dragon-folk dead, not to mention to take over our fertile lands. Rumor had it that the majority of the Nightfall lands were hot and desolate in the summer months, and nothing grew there.

"You can do this," Joslyn encouraged me. I could hear the shakiness in her voice.

She'd been there to witness my fall, seeing me lying broken and bleeding on the ground. At night, when I lay down to sleep, I could sometimes still hear her screams for help in my head.

The king stepped up to me, forcing me to meet his gaze. "I will fly under you so that if you fall I can catch you."

Looking into his green eyes, hearing his promise, it made my stomach warm. I instantly felt guilty for these feelings, especially with Joslyn right here. The heat between our bodies was so intense that he stepped backwards. This happened often between us but we said nothing about it, ignoring it.

"Fine," I growled. "But if I break a single bone, you owe me five hundred jade coins."

He grinned. "Deal."

"I would have gone for a thousand," Joslyn told me as I walked over and handed her my sword, coin purse, and belt.

I smiled at her. "Your bones are far more valuable than mine," I informed her, and then walked towards the creek where the brush was thick, so that I could change in privacy.

The king simply faced a tree and began to disrobe out in the open. That man didn't care who saw him naked, and I was again currently transfixed by a view of his butt cheeks. With a chuckle, I peeled off my training clothes, which were covered in mud from my sparring session with Cal earlier, and when I stood fully naked I looked down at my body.

A variety of purple, blue, and yellowing bruises marred my hips and knees. I was proud of every single one of them. The muscled indentations in my stomach and thighs were the most pronounced and I was proud of that too.

Closing my eyes, I took in a deep breath and felt for my magic.

Transforming, as the king had taught me, was a different compartment of magic than throwing or breathing fire. It was deeper, and needed to really be pulled out with confidence. Reaching for my transformation magic, I pulled on it hard with as much strength as I could muster. Pain laced along my spine and I hunched forward as the sound of cracking bones began to ring throughout the bushes.

"He's already done!" Joslyn trilled.

"Well, he has to wait!" I bellowed back in a painful growl.

The king was an impatient man, I'd learned, but that only made me want to make him wait longer on me.

After I finished my transformation, I stepped out of the thick bushes, breaking some of the branches on my way.

'Perfect day for flying,' the king said when he saw me.

I gave him the equivalent of a dragon snort and eyeroll. *'Remember, my Royal Guard contract states that if I die, you must bring my body back to my mother in Cinder Village.'*

He chuffed, '*I would never let that happen, Arwen.*'

I sidled next to him, giving him a long side look. '*Now you care whether I live or die? You've come along way, my king.*'

A month ago, he'd imprisoned me and threatened to kill me. I was determined to never let him live that down.

'*I told you, I regretted my actions from when we first met. I thought you were here to kill me!*' he snapped.

Shooting my wings open, I pumped them as I fast as I could. '*Nope, just a girl from Cinder Village who can't fly!*' I kicked off the ground at the last word before I could lose my nerve.

Terror shot through me as the wind resistance pushed against my wings. I faltered, but Drae's voice was in my head to comfort me.

'*You're doing great, just breathe and focus on your wingbeats.*'

I sucked air in through my dragon nostrils and then looked down to see Drae directly under me.

'*I'll catch you if you fall.*'

Shaking my nerves off, I focused on what his wings were doing. Up, pause, down, pause, up, pause. I mimicked what we were doing, which was a lot slower, smoother, and controlled than my frantic fast flying.

'That's it,' he said.

"Go, Arwen!" Joslyn's voice from down below reached me and I grinned.

Drae veered to the left, heading for the farmland outside the palace gates, and I swallowed.

'Are you sure?' I asked him.

Only select members of the Royal Guard and house staff knew about my transformation powers. To fly over farms would get people talking. Only a full-blooded royal dragon could transform.

'I'm prepared to address questions about you and your abilities,' was all he said as we flew over the castle gates.

I'd never flown this far, or this long, but I pushed away my anxiety and followed him. We glided over rows and rows of wheat, then the golden fields turned to purple lavender, and finally he began to descend over a group of willow trees.

We were maybe a half hour walk from the castle. It had been a nice short flight. Not too long for me, but just enough that I felt confident and wanted more. As we lowered, I peered down to see where he was taking us and my heart leapt into my throat.

Between the circle of four giant weeping willows

were a handful of gravestones. One was large, as you would have for an adult, and the other four were small.

Four children.

This was where Queen Amelia and his unborn children lay.

'I don't know why I brought you here,' he said suddenly in my head as he landed before the small graves. A basket of clothes was beneath one of the trees, and I wondered if it was because he flew here often and then shifted into human form.

I swallowed hard, landing roughly next to him, trying not to fall over as landing was not yet something I had mastered.

I didn't know what to say yet, so I just stood beside him, staring at the solid green jade headstone with gold engraved writing.

Her Majesty, Queen Amelia.
Beloved wife and mother.
Best Friend.

A sob formed in my throat, but it sounded like a hacking growl in my dragon form.

The king looked over at me, his black shiny scales in such contrast to his yellow burning eyes. *'Don't try to cry in dragon form. It sounds awful and will scare the local villagers nearby.'*

He rarely joked with me, so it startled me and I

snort-laughed, which again sounded awful in dragon form. Black smoke leaked from my nostrils.

His lips peeled back, displaying all of his dragon teeth. I was hoping it was a smile and not that he wanted to eat me for laughing at a time like this.

'Amelia would have liked you. She liked to practice her sword with Regina any chance she got.'

'Really?' I asked, I never knew that about her. I'd only ever seen her in a dress with a delicate wave and feminine makeup. Imagining her practicing sword with Regina brought a smile to my lips.

'After we lost our first child, Amelia ran from the castle crying and I found her here, in the center of the trees weeping. I asked her to come back and that I would build a mausoleum for our lost little one that was bigger than a house, but she said no.'

'Why?' I stepped closer to him, hanging on his every word.

'She said that the trees looked like they were crying too, and she wanted to share her grief with them to lessen the burden. So we buried our first one here.'

My chest ached as sorrow overcame me. It was a beautiful thing to say. The trees did indeed look like they were crying, hence the name "weeping willow."

What he didn't have to say was that another child

passed, and another, and finally another, along with his wife. And he'd brought them all out here.

'Thank you for bringing me here. It is a very special place.'

He started to shift into his human form then and I turned, giving him privacy as he put on clothes. Walking over to a field of wildflowers, he pulled a handful of them and placed them on Amelia's grave. Then he pulled another bunch and I decided to shift as well. Shifting back into my human form felt like pulling the plug on a bathtub drain. You were holding everything in and suddenly it all rushed out. It took me a moment to transform, then I ran over to the basket, putting on a long tunic that hung past my knees and smelled of Drae. It hung well past my knees so I didn't bother with the trousers.

Drae was laying flowers on the third child's grave when I pulled a bunch of purple and white blooms, bunching them together, and then met him at the fourth. Without a word, I handed them to him and he placed them on top of the little mound.

We stood there quiet for a long time, just letting the light breeze move the long ropelike branches of the willow, until finally he turned to me with a storm brewing in his gaze.

"I don't love Joslyn," he declared, and my entire body went rigid.

Why was he telling me that? Because I was now good friends with her?

"I respect her, I care for her well-being... but I don't love her."

My heart rattled my ribs like a cage. I genuinely feared it would leap out of my chest and fall onto the ground, exposing my nerves.

"You must have an heir or the dragon-folk people would die." I tried to assuage his guilt and he nodded.

"But I could have chosen you," he said boldly, stepping closer to me, and it was like the entire world had been tipped on its axis.

Why is he saying this? My brain was so befuddled I didn't even know how to respond. Was he saying he wished he had picked me? Simultaneous excitement and sorrow ripped through me. The king took another step closer. My breast pressed against his chest with only a thin piece of cloth between us and suddenly it felt as if I had stepped into an inferno. Heat like I'd never felt before rushed through me and my upper lip broke out in a sweat. He took in a deep breath, his chest pressing harder against me, and then exhaled a shuddering breath. He leaned forward, licking his lips to wet them.

I wanted to kiss him—Hades, I wanted to bed him right now, but there was one thing flashing through my mind in this moment.

Joslyn.

He might not love her, but *she* was falling in love with him. They might not be married yet and it might only be a marriage of convenience, but I couldn't do that to her. She was my friend.

I turned my face quickly. "I can't," I muttered, and he froze, taking a giant step back from me and pulling all of that delicious warmth with him.

Swallowing hard, he nodded, a conflicted look washing over his face. "Maybe this is for the best. If I don't love anyone, then they can't destroy me when they die." He spun, stepping out of the circle of weeping willows.

Emotion tightened my throat to the point of causing me pain as I worked hard not to cry. I wanted to run to him, pull him into my arms and tell him he could love me. That it would be safe, that I would love him back. But surrounded by those loved ones he'd watched die, I just wasn't sure it was the truth. Like Dr. Elsie had said, we didn't know what kind of child our pairing would create—Joslyn was the safer choice. While I was collecting myself, he tossed off his clothes and gave me another view of his royal ass.

I groaned, hating the perfect detail of his butt cheeks, and then spun to give him my back. I yanked off the tunic in anger and then started my own shift.

Why did he do that? Why did he say that?

I don't love Joslyn.

I could have chosen you.

Those words would haunt me until my dying day.

When I was fully shifted into my dragon form, I turned around and he took one look at me and kicked off the ground, heading for the sky.

I followed him, still dumbfounded at his confession. Did he regret not choosing me? Did he want to change his mind? I wanted to know, but I decided to say nothing. For Joslyn's sake. For all dragon-folks' sake.

He made his bed and he was going to have to lie in it.

The flight back was quiet and slightly awkward. Drae flew below me just as he promised, and with each beat of my wings the fear of flying left me. When we made it back to the training field, Joslyn was there, ever the good betrothed, waiting on her man in her new yellow dress.

Guilt wormed through me at the sight of her excitedly waving at us.

"You did it!" she screamed.

I don't love Joslyn.

"Go, Arwen!" She pumped her fist into the air.

I don't love Joslyn.

I snuck off into the bushes and changed, feeling the ball in my stomach growing heavier and heavier. When I stepped out, Joslyn was pulling a leaf out of the king's hair and smiling up at him.

"Do you want to have dinner together tonight?" Joslyn asked him.

"I have... a lot of work to catch up on," he said, looking at me guiltily.

My heart simultaneously broke for Joslyn, and cheered that the king didn't love her. It was horrible, evil, and yet I realized in that moment that I wanted him for myself. I wished he'd chosen me, but that kind of daydreaming would eat away at a person. Not to mention Joslyn was my dear friend and this wasn't right. I needed to remedy it immediately.

It wasn't fair to Joslyn.

Walking in a rush, I took off for the horse barn in search of Cal, telling Joslyn and the king I had somewhere I needed to be. Cal had been flirting with me for three weeks straight. I would kiss him and we would both see that we could be happy together and I could forget about the king. Drae in turn would see me with another man and then move on happily with Joslyn. It was a win-win.

Passing droves of soldiers, I screamed Cal's name and finally found him saddling his horse on the side of the barn.

He looked up with a grin when he saw me approach. "You still sore from that—?"

I crashed into him, pressing my lips to his. His arms came around me, pulling me closer to him. He groaned as our lips touched and I immediately felt the gravity of my mistake.

The world did not tilt on its axis. This kiss was not earth-shattering. It felt like I was kissing my mother goodnight.

He pulled away abruptly, looking at me with wide eyes, as if he too did not enjoy the kiss.

I was such an idiot. I prayed that the Maker would strike me dead with a lightning bolt right then and there so that I didn't have to experience this.

"Sorry," I muttered, stumbling away from him. "I... have no idea what I was thinking."

He reached out and took my hand. "No. Don't be... I want to but... I'm not allowed."

I stilled, his fingers in mine as I stared up at him. "You're not *allowed* to kiss me?"

He cheeks pinked and he looked left and right as if

making sure no one was close enough to hear us. "The king has told the entire Royal Guard that none of us may have you."

That. Bastard.

"Why?" My heart hammered in my chest. I could physically feel the color draining from my face.

Cal chewed on his bottom lip. "In case something happens to Joslyn... you're his backup."

Actual bile crept up my throat. The king ordered none of the Royal Guard to like me so that he could keep me on the side as a *backup?*

I was *no one's* backup.

That *bastard.*

I nodded, walking briskly away from Cal as he called my name. Tears started to well up but I blinked them back.

Don't let them see you cry.

I'd been training nearly a month. I'd broken bones, cut myself, been knocked out, and not shed a single tear in front of these men. I would not cry now over an invisible heart wound.

Passing Annabeth, I gave her a curt smile, my throat tightening the faster I walked. When I finally pulled the door to my quarters open, I threw myself inside and then slammed it shut behind me.

"Arwen?" Narine's sweet voice came from the

kitchen and then everything broke inside of me. Sobs wracked my body as I crumpled to the floor. I couldn't hold it together anymore.

"Oh Maker." Narine rushed forward, picking me up and scanning my body as if looking for wounds. "You hurt?"

"Not physically." I sniffled. "I never wanted to come here! I didn't want to marry him. I didn't ask for any of this." I wept.

Understanding dawned on Narine's expression and she nodded, her curls bouncing around her face. "Matters of the heart hurt more than bodily injuries. I'll make you some tea and run a bath."

"Thank you," I whimpered, allowing her to take me to the couch and deposit me there.

The longer I sat there, sipping my tea as Narine ran the bath, the angrier I became. Drae proposed to Joslyn, he chose her, he should not be making passes at me. And then telling the Royal Guard not to touch me so I could be his backup! It wasn't fair. I wanted to punch him right in his pretty little face!

"You're smoking," Narine said, and I froze, looking down at the curls of smoke floating up from my nose.

Taking a deep breath, I calmed myself.

If I don't love anyone, then they can't destroy me when

they die. The king's haunting words came to me then and I deflated. All anger at him fled from me and just became a ball of sorrow and pity. He was in a horrible position, bound by duty for his people. Joslyn was the safer choice for him to have a child with and I respected that. If the situation were reversed, I would have made the same choice—denying my heart for the betterment of my people.

After my bath, I read for a while and then planned to turn in early when there was a knock at the door. I hoped it was the king, but by the lateness of the hour it would be inappropriate.

When Narine pulled the door back, Joslyn stepped inside, red blotchy eyes the hallmark sign that she had been crying.

Hades.

"Can you go for a walk?" she asked.

No.

"Sure." I slipped into my sandals, and tucked my hunting knife into the back waistband of my trousers out of habit.

We were quiet walking down the hallway. I waved to a passing maid and then to the Royal Guard stationed at the door that led out to the gardens. Only when we were alone in the garden, peering at the purple lilacs, did Joslyn look at me.

"He will never love me," she said and my heart broke.

"What?" I tried to act surprised.

Joslyn wrung her hands together. "I just spoke to him. He made it clear this will be a marriage of convenience and he isn't sure he will ever love me as I deserve to be loved, and he told me I can get out of it if I want."

Shock ran through me at that. "Get out of it? End the betrothal?"

She nodded. "He said he would make sure my family name was not tarnished if I chose to walk away. I would still have highborn status and he would pay a monthly stipend to take care of me for the rest of my life."

My heart pinched at the king's kindness. I blinked back tears several times as my vision blurred. "What are you going to do?"

She chewed her lip. "I'm going to stay. It's my duty to provide a royal heir and save the people of Embergate and so I'll do it. Love or not."

So he also told her about needing an heir to save his people. Her people. Our people. Ninety percent of the people in Embergate carried dragon magic in their veins and would succumb to death as the king's magic eventually faded away.

I was suddenly flooded with so much respect for Joslyn. "You're a good person. You'll make a wonderful queen," I informed her.

I pulled her into a hug and she wept on my shoulder. I'd be lying if I didn't admit that my heart broke for the fact that I would never have Drae to myself. But I vowed right then and there to never again see the king as an object of desire. Out of respect for Joslyn, who clearly loved him.

When she pulled back, she wiped her eyes. "Tell me a story. Take my mind off of this."

I nodded, starting to pace the garden, trying to think up a story from my childhood that would make her laugh. "When I was young, my father had just died and we didn't have coal for the fireplace. Ironic considering where we live, but coal had to be bought just like everything else. Without my father's wages, my mother feared it would be a terrible and cold winter."

Joslyn looked at me with concern. "What did you do?"

"Well," I murmured, pacing the grass, "I had heard that the people of Gypsy Rock kept warm by burning dried cow dung patties... except we didn't have any cows in Cinder Village. Only dogs."

Joslyn suddenly burst into laughter. "You didn't!"

I grinned, turning to face her, delighted that I'd

gotten her to laugh and lifted her spirits. "I am happy to report that dog shit burns pretty hot when—"

The words died in my throat. A man suddenly appeared behind Joslyn. His one hand went around her mouth and his other held a knife to her throat. He wore the Nightfall crest on his armor. The glint of steel from his mechanical wings flickered in the moonlight.

I stood there shocked for a split second and then reached for my knife at the back of my shirt. Then leaves rustled behind me and someone grasped my wrist, clenching it hard until I dropped the blade.

"Not so fast," a male voice like scratchy wool said.

My heart hammered in my throat as I looked at a terrified and shaking Joslyn.

"Which one is the wife-to-be?" the man holding Joslyn asked whoever held me.

Small tendrils of smoke leaked from my nostrils and I pulled on my dragon power.

The male behind me squeezed my hand tighter, immobilizing me. "Yours."

It happened so fast.

One second Joslyn was standing upright and the next the man was dragging the blade across her throat and her life blood was dribbling all down her gown before her body hit the floor.

"Take that one too. She's the backup." A man I recognized stepped out of the woods.

Bonner. A Royal Guardsman. A traitor.

I'd never liked him.

The man holding me pulled out his blade. The crushing grief and realization that Joslyn was dead slammed into me, tearing me in two.

An inhuman wail ripped from my throat as heat, and rage, and anguish, consumed me. A burst of blue fire exploded outward, and then everything went black.

"Arwen." A familiar panicked voice roused me. "Arwen!" There was a light slap on my cheek.

My eyelids sprang open and I came face to face with Drae.

His panicked green gaze ran the length of my body. "Are you hurt?" he said.

I blinked a few times and then looked down to see that I was completely naked. My clothes had burned off. Little bits of ash and soot stained my skin. My gaze peered out around the garden, and the memory of everything came back to me.

"Joslyn," I whimpered, my lip quivering as my body started to shake.

The king reached down and pulled off his tunic, and then helped me sit up, threading my arms through the garment. Soldiers ran around the garden barking orders and taking up arms, but all I could see was the beautiful dark hair splayed out on the grass and the puddle of blood under Joslyn's body.

"I... I couldn't save her," I sobbed.

The king hauled me up into his arms and I peered down at two corpses. They were burned like animal meat. I must have... my power...

"Someone betrayed me. Who was it?" the king growled as he walked with me in his arms, tucking me tightly to his chest.

"Bonner," I croaked.

The king's jaw ticked and his arms pulled tighter around me. As we passed Cal, the king stopped to face him. "Take Bonner's wife in for interrogation. If she knew he was a traitor, banish her and their children to Nightfall."

Cal nodded and then took off running.

Nightfall was no place for dragon-folk... I guess that was why the king would ban traitors there. The second you stepped foot on their soil, they killed you if you had an ounce of magical blood in you. I didn't care about that right now. I couldn't get the image of Joslyn being bled like a goat in out of my mind.

My body shivered as a deathly cold crept over me.

Drae slapped my cheek and I gasped, realizing I'd blacked out again.

"She's going into shock," Dr. Elsie said.

When did Dr. Elsie get here?

I peered around, looking at the black dragon scale-patterned wallpaper and dark gray lacquered four-poster bed. Drae deposited me on the charcoal silk sheets and stared down at me, wide-eyed. "She burned up half the garden, exploded with dragon fire at least twenty feet wide."

Dr. Elsie pulled an elven healing wand from her doctor's bag and held it over me. I'd seen an elven healing one time. An elf came through town while traveling the perilous Narrow Strait, the small bit of neutral land in Nightfall territory that led from Embergate to Thorngate. One toe outside of the strait and the Nightfall warriors would stick an arrow in your back with legal right.

The elf had been traveling with a friend who'd strayed outside of the neutral portion of the Narrow Strait and he'd shown up to Cinder Village with an arrow in his back. When the healer had brought her healing wand out, I'd never forgotten the unearthly glow it held. It was a cross between blue and purple but also silver. It was like the stars in the sky were contained in that wand and...

Slap.

I gasped, my eyelids fluttering open.

"Stay with me!" Dr. Elsie bellowed.

"Stop slapping me," I whimpered weakly, looking up at her.

"I need you conscious, Arwen. You're going into shock and I don't know why."

Her words scared the life out of me.

She held the wand now, as small as a stick you would pick up to float downriver. It glowed that magical blueish purple and the light seemed to bathe my skin, wrapping around it and hugging my body. The light didn't touch the sheets beneath me, it only seemed to search out and stick to that which was alive, the same way it had the fallen elf who'd been brought to my village.

My legs suddenly started to shake, and my teeth chattered violently.

Elsie gasped, looking at the light that bathed my skin as if it had just told her something. "Run a hot bath! She's cold as ice. Organs shutting down. She used

249

all of her fire to fight off the men and now she's... freezing to death."

King Valdren loomed over me now, eyes glowing with orange fire. "There's no time for a bath. Move."

Dr. Elsie glanced up at him with a frown. "My lord, she needs hea—"

"MOVE!" he bellowed and she leapt to her feet, stumbling backwards.

My entire body convulsed, the coldness creeping into my very heart and squeezing. I closed my eyes, ready to meet the Maker, then a searing heat washed over my skin. My eyelids snapped open just as the king lowered himself on top of me, flames shooting from his hands and encompassing my entire body.

It *burned*, but in a good way. His hands reached under me and then he pulled me to him, smooshing us together in this cocoon of heat. The flames danced around us and I smelled smoke as the bedding singed, but the king and I remained unharmed, as if this dragon fire were a healing balm and not the scorching heat it would be to someone else. I stared up into his eyes, feeling the weight of him on top of me as he looked down.

The realization hit me hard.

I'd fallen in love with him. I wanted him. I...

Emotion tightened my throat as I thought of Joslyn.

Of Cal and how he wouldn't kiss me. I was the backup —he didn't choose me. I needed to remember that.

The heat thawed the deep cold that had taken over me and my body stopped its shivering. My teeth no longer chattered, and clarity returned to my mind. I took in a deep breath, no longer feeling only half in this world.

The fire around us died down and Regina and Dr. Elsie rushed forward, patting the sheets to put out the small fires that had erupted around us. The king pushed off of me, chest heaving, naked as the day he was born.

His eyes hooded as he gazed down at me. I peered at my body to see that the tunic had burned off and I was again completely naked as well.

"Keep her safe," he told Dr. Elsie. "She doesn't leave my room until I'm back."

Dr. Elsie nodded and Drae crossed the room, grabbing a pair of trousers from the wardrobe. Regina sidled up beside him. "My king, how will you retaliate for this injustice? The queen of Nightfall just killed your betrothed and then tried to kill your backup."

Backup.

She said *backup.* So Regina knew too? Was I the only one who truly thought I was here because he wanted me to be in his army? I rolled onto my side, away from them; the tears fell down my cheeks and onto the burnt sheets. Dr. Elsie spread a new blanket over me and began to scan me again with the elven wand.

"She took my opportunity of an heir, so now I'll take one of hers." The king's voice could cut glass and I stiffened at his words.

"One of her sons?" Regina sounded pleased.

The king must have nodded, because then the door slammed and I was left in silence, bathed in the elven healing light and all alone.

The king was going to kill one of the Nightfall queen's sons? I heard she had seven, and one daughter.

What if Drae got killed trying to retaliate for Joslyn's death? I couldn't let that happen, not when I had the power to help them.

I sat up, causing Dr. Elsie to lean backwards to avoid cracking heads with me.

"Am I healed? His fire healed me, right? I feel fine," I informed her, and by fine I meant physically fine and emotionally fragile.

She frowned. "Your body looks stable, organs functioning as planned, but—"

I leapt off the bed and ran to the king's wardrobe.

"But you cannot go anywhere. King's orders!" Elsie demanded.

I threw on one of his tunics, not bothering with underclothes, and burst out the door.

"Ooph." I ran right into Cal's chest.

"I can't let you go anywhere," he told me, frowning as he took in my appearance. I probably had soot in my hair and the creases of my skin and looked like a wild animal. I didn't care. I felt like one.

"Move," I growled, my nostrils smoking.

Cal rolled his eyes, widening his stance. "By order of the king, you will not leave this room, Arwen."

I raised my hand, calling a ball of fire into it. "Back up, or escort me to Drae. I don't care which, but get out of my way."

Cal sighed, stepping out of the way. "I'll escort you to him and then right back here," he said.

I took off running, not bothering to wait.

If the king was going to seek revenge in Joslyn's name, then I was going to help him.

I knew where he would be—in the stables preparing to ride with his army. I ran through the hallway, my legs still shaky from the trauma of seeing Joslyn killed right in front of me. I couldn't get the image of her body lying in the puddle of crimson blood out of my head. Streaking across the grassy pathway to the barn, I found him addressing a small contingent of six Drayken guards, Regina included.

"I'll shift forms and fly two of you on my back into Nightfall territory—"

When he saw me approach, he stopped talking. "Arwen," he growled, and then looked to Cal.

"I'm going," I demanded.

Regina sighed, whisking away the five other guards, plus Cal, and then it was just Drae and I.

"You cannot go. This is not up for discussion," he announced.

I narrowed my eyes at him and stepped closer until our toes were nearly touching. "I'm not staying back here to be your safe little *backup*," I spat. "I'm more than my womb. I'm a warrior, and I'll fight for Joslyn's honor with or without you!"

His head reeled back as if I'd slapped him. "I... I don't see you simply as a womb, nor just a *backup*," he growled.

"Lies," I snapped. "That's all you've seen of me from day one. Joslyn too. She was going to stay with you, you know that? She mentioned to me in the garden that even though you told her you would never love her, that she would stay and do her duty to give you an heir."

He froze, his breaths coming in and out in ragged gasps. "I told Joslyn I wouldn't love her... because I've fallen for another," he said.

I went very still, my heart beating so fast I thought it might jump out onto the ground and show him how nervous I was.

"Who?" I asked timidly, praying I knew the answer.

"You. I want *you*," he pressed.

I gulped, everything inside of me warring with the other. *Joslyn. Backup. Kissing Cal. Royal womb. Heir. Backup. Backup. Backup.*

"You don't want me. You *need* me—you need my womb," I clarified, unable to get over the truth of the matter. If Joslyn weren't dead right now, and I weren't his only option at a child, would he still be saying all this?

"You are an impossible woman!" he screamed, lunging for me.

I stumbled backwards, thinking for a wild second that he might hit me. I should have known better. His hand came around the back of my neck and then he yanked me forward, pressing his lips to mine.

I gasped, inhaling his breath. My lips opened and our tongues crashed together. Our kisses always seemed to be this way, angry, passionate, and feverish. His other hand came around my lower back and he pressed my stomach into him. I moaned at the feeling of his body flush with mine; heat built between us, and I slipped my tongue across his, feeling the world tilt.

There was a hungriness to his kiss that I loved. It was like he was starved for my taste and couldn't get enough. I wanted to consume him all the same but one word kept playing out in my head.

Backup.

Was he only kissing me now that Joslyn was dead and I was his only chance at an heir? Did I blame him? Did I still want his affections if they were fake?

I pulled away from him, no longer drunk on his lips, and reached up to grab my mouth.

His brows dipped in concern as he watched me.

"I respect the position you are in but..." I took a deep breath. "I'm too good to be anyone's backup plan." I held my chin high, knowing full well that this might get me killed. This could have been the only reason he was keeping me alive, and now that I was denying him, he would do what my mother warned all along.

He grabbed his chest as if I'd stuck a blade in it. "Arwen, you're... you don't understand—"

"My lord!" Regina's sharp voice came from behind us both and I jumped. "Morning light approaches. If we want to do this and get home under the cover of darkness, we must go now."

I looked to Drae. "I'm flying. I can carry one on my back." The only sane way into Nightfall territory was by air. Their borders were the most secure in all the realms.

His eyes glowed orange. "You've never carried anyone before."

"I'm small," Regina said, "she can carry me. I know how to remain still and not throw her off balance."

"It's settled," I stated, and walked into the barn past the king to take off his tunic I was wearing and shift.

They argued a little outside but I didn't care. I *was* going. I felt even more guilty now for kissing the king before Joslyn's body had barely been dead an hour. I had to seek revenge. When I was fully shifted, I stepped out of the barn and into the open pasture, where the king had also shifted into his dragon form. I gasped as I noticed the small patches of human skin peeking through his black scales, as if he couldn't fully shift.

"It's getting worse," Regina noted, and I froze, the gravity of seeing him like that weighing on me.

His magic was dying without an heir—something I could give him. Something I *wanted* to give him. He looked at me and I felt an intangible bond form between us. It was hard to explain but it was as if something knitted together, tying my fate to his.

Maker help me, I prayed. Where Drae was concerned I was sure of nothing, only that I wanted to be true to myself first and foremost. I wanted to be loved, adored, wanted.

'Let's fly,' he said. 'For Joslyn.'

'For Joslyn,' I agreed.

I kicked off the ground and flew west with my mind replaying the best kiss I'd ever had in my life. Would every kiss with him be like that? Was it just because it was new and exciting and... forbidden? I shouldn't be kissing a betrothed king. *A king who is now mourning the loss of his future wife.*

But was he mourning? He didn't seem to be. He respected Joslyn but he seemed angrier about her death than sad. Still, it was inappropriate timing and I felt awful. Why would I kiss a man who said nothing when Regina called me the backup? That was the biggest reason of all not to kiss him ever again. These thoughts warred in my mind as we flew towards a fate unknown.

W e flew low over the Nightfall border, hiding within a dense bed of fog. I'd never been to this part of the realm before, and although I was on a mission I was also sightseeing in a way. Once we reached their main gate, we flew higher into the sky to avoid their detection.

The Nightfall realm had more glass and metal than I had seen in my entire life. Mechanical horseless carriages with lamps in front of them rolled down the streets. And even though it was nighttime, everything was lit up. But there was no flame or fire, it was... a different type of light. A soft, constant glow. The buildings were expertly made. Glass, brick, and metal. All the lines were straight, nothing looked jagged or pieced-together hastily. I regretted to admit it was beautiful, a sight to behold.

Soldiers were stationed everywhere, two on every corner, and they all held different killing contraptions. Metal weapons with projectiles loaded into them. Arrow throwers, spear throwers, and one even had a flame burning from the tip. Fire thrower?

What was this place? A place of invention and technology the likes of which I couldn't imagine in my wildest dreams... or nightmares. It was as if the queen wanted to expunge the realm of magic and then use her machines and metal to become *magical humans*.

'The queen's beloved eldest son lives outside Nightfall Castle in his own fort.' Drae's voice pierced my mind, pulling me from my thoughts.

'How do you know?' I asked as we veered left, away from the bright lights of a far-off castle and towards a smaller village.

'Spies,' was all he said.

The kiss we'd shared lingered between us. I didn't know how to act in front of him now. He'd saved my life by heating me up when I'd been freezing, but I didn't feel thankful. I felt angry that he told Cal and all of the other guards not to date me. He casually accepted Regina's referral to me as his backup, and then just so casually mentioned that he wanted me within minutes of Joslyn's death. Did he refer to me as a backup with Regina and not a member of his Royal Guard, not a friend? Because that's what hurt the most.

I was an insurance policy.

Smoke began to leak from my nostrils and the king's black head swiveled in my direction. I snuffed out the fire and faced forward, ready to just focus on the task at hand.

Avenge Joslyn.

It still didn't feel real, that she was gone, that her soul had left her body.

'*I should have protected her. What a lousy Royal Guard I make,*' I muttered to Drae.

He peered over at me. '*Lousy Royal Guard? What about the dozen guards the Nightfall soldiers passed when they broke into my palace? Regina is beside herself that she didn't do her job. You did more than anyone. You killed them.*'

I hadn't thought of how Regina might be taking this. How upset she would be that as the leader of the Drayken she allowed two outsiders to break in and kill the king's betrothed. Not to mention the fact that she'd had a spy within her ranks and never knew.

I kept quiet after that, realizing that this affected more than just me. Though I was confident that out of everyone, I knew Joslyn the best and cared for her the most.

'*Go low, into that mist,*' the king said suddenly, and dropped. I lowered myself with him and then we were flying in a damp white haze.

"That outcrop of trees..." Regina said.

I peered to the left to see that just inside the fort's gates was a small orchard. We stayed in the mist, passing over the fence, and then when we were directly over the trees Drae dropped suddenly, as if his wings had broken.

'*Drop quickly so that you aren't seen, and then pump your wings last minute to lessen the impact,*' the king said.

Fear gripped me at such a fall. It reminded me of the time the wind had tumbled me to the ground and I'd been severely injured.

I circled the orchard, still hidden in the mist, terror consuming me. What if I didn't fall fast enough and the guards saw us? Or what if I fell too fast and then I killed Regina, who was attached to a basket on my back? I circled for a good minute, tearing myself in two with anxiety, when Regina reached out and stroked my head. "You got this. I'll be okay. I've tumbled and dove from King Valdren's back many times."

With that assurance, I dropped, collapsing my wings so that we were in a dead freefall. Instinct had me wanting to flap my wings to stay airborne, but Drae's voice boomed in my mind:

'Hold.'

The second I cleared the top of the trees, my wings burst from my back in panic.

'Now!' Drae cried, and I flapped like crazy to slow my descent. I did slow, but it was still a fast fall, and my feet and chest crashed into the earth as I stumbled forward like a drunken buffoon at a midsummer festival. I felt Regina teeter on top of me, then I was able to regain my balance.

Regina made quick work of unhooking my saddle, and then held out my brown leather hunting suit. The king had already changed and was waiting for me with three men, Cal included. Nox and Falcon were the other two. Falcon was an old timer with so many scars I didn't know how his skin moved at all. He'd been burned in a fire, that's all I knew. I'd learned that he'd also had a pet falcon which gave him the name, but it had since died. He was a good man, and the king's very loyal friend who served under his father.

"Regina," Drae whispered, "we will break up into two teams." He spoke while I changed and the men gave me their backs for privacy. "Falcon, Nox, and I will go in first. You and Arwen and Cal will bring up the rear and be the extraction team."

I knew from my training that meant I might have to prepare a way to get them out after they carried out the assassination. It was the easier of the two jobs, but he'd let me come, so I wasn't going to complain. I finished dressing, and walked up beside him.

"Killing this guy will hurt the queen?" I whispered to Drae. I wanted to make sure that witch paid for what she'd done to my friend.

Drae nodded. "Not only that, he's her lead commander. No mission goes through without his planning and approval."

I grit my jaw, feeling my teeth creak at the pressure. This guy was directly responsible for Joslyn's death?

I looked over at Drae. "Promise me you'll take him out."

He peered over at me and nodded. "You have my word, Arwen."

Arwen. The way he said my name made my stomach twist into knots.

We snuck into a side alleyway and let the king

265

lead. He was holding a paper map and consulting it often. Whoever his spy was had given us a diagram that led right to the sleeping chambers of the Nightfall queen's eldest son.

Her heir.

The gravity of what we were about to do settled into me. Killing a man while he slept, no matter how evil he was, was hard to stomach. I knew now why Drae put me on the extraction team. I wouldn't be there to see it, and after witnessing Joslyn's death only hours ago I was grateful.

We reached the side of a large estate, hiding in the alley, and immediately shrank into the shadows as a guard passed by ahead. The guard was bathed in lantern light, and I was relieved to see that he didn't have the metal wings attached to him.

There was a small window on the side of the house just ahead. Drae made a signal with his fingers to Regina and she nodded. I peered closer to see that it was cracked open! He was going in that window, and then I wouldn't see him until it was over.

What if Drae died...? What if the queen's son slept with a sword under his pillow and a guard at his door?

Reaching for Drae's hand before he could walk away, I squeezed it.

'Be safe,' I sent mentally, unsure if it would work in

human form.

He nodded to me, squeezing my hand back, and then left, Falcon and Nox following him.

I was pissed at the bastard right now, but I didn't want him to die. I couldn't handle another death.

Without speaking, Regina made a hand signal for Cal and I to follow her to the end of the alleyway. By the time we passed the open window, Drae and the others had already slipped inside.

When we got to the end of the alley, Regina pointed across the street to the stables, and Cal and I nodded. That was where we needed to get to. There was a good chance Drae would end up injured and then we'd have to horse and carriage our way home somehow. Either way, we needed two exits at all times, one by sky and one by land. Just in case.

Regina peeked her head out into the alleyway and looked left and right quickly. She sucked her body back into the shadows and then gave the go signal.

The three of us walked briskly out from the alleyway and towards the stables. Not a full sprint, which would be suspicious to an observer, but not slow enough to be unusual either. It was the perfect walk of three friends trying to hurry home in the late hour after a night of drinking at the tavern.

The second we entered the stables, a guard was

there. He'd been relieving himself inside, and at the sight of us he yanked his pants upward. Fumbling, he tried to reach for his sword, but Regina was faster. She lunged, and with the butt of her dagger cracked him on the side of the head. He crumpled into a puddle of his own urine.

"That's unfortunate," Regina said softly. We then made quick work with the horses. I hadn't yet taken proper riding lessons, but part of my pup training meant I'd had to muck out the stalls and tie the saddles, so I knew how to do that now. Within minutes we had two large mares hooked up to a medium-sized wagon that should hold all of us. We couldn't find a closed-top carriage; they were all mechanical here, horseless, and we didn't know how to work them. But the wagon, which looked like it hadn't been used in years, would do. Regina had laid some blankets inside that we could use to take cover if needed. My heart raced as I thought of the king inside the estate right now, carrying out an assassination attempt on the Nightfall queen's son. It was brazen and dangerous—but necessary.

For Joslyn.

If the queen thought she could just waltz into Embergate and take out the king's chance at having an heir, she was sorely mistaken.

We kept the horses just inside the stable, waiting

for a signal from Drae that he needed extraction.

Instead of a signal, the front door of the house blew off its hinges and Drae was tossed out onto the street in a puff of black smoke.

What the...?

Regina kicked the horse with her heels as chaos erupted into the once silent night. Nox and Falcon burst from the home next, each bleeding from their arms. Half a dozen guards followed them with swords drawn.

I barely had time to process the scene when Regina whisked the wagon beside them and whistled.

The king, Falcon, and Nox launched themselves inside and then we took off.

"Mission accomplished," was all Drae said and a triumphant feeling spread throughout my limbs. They did it. The person responsible for Joslyn's death was dead.

A loud and deep horn blew throughout the fort and I knew they'd be shutting the gates and preparing for an attack. An arrow whizzed past my head and I ducked before popping up again, wide-eyed. *This must be what war felt like*, I thought. By the time you processed what was going on, another situation entirely had unfolded.

"Hold the reins," Regina told me.

I scrambled onto the horse as Regina switched places with me and grabbed her bow, shooting arrows at the approaching army of angry Nightfall soldiers running after us.

"Arwen, let's fly!" Drae cried out.

My heart hammered in my chest as the horses barreled for the fort's closed gates. Shift into a dragon and fly out of here while riding on a moving horse! *Is he insane?*

I spun to find him already ripping off his shirt.

Hades, he is serious. Here we go...

Abandoning the reins, I jumped into the small wagon with him, yanking off my leathers without a care for nakedness. Who could worry about exposing oneself when you were about to die?

The king was the first to strip down, but only half-way, still wearing trousers, and within seconds he sprouted wings from his back with a growl of pain. He'd transformed into a partial dragon, wings only, and then used his arms to grab Nox and Falcon by the waist.

"Can you take Cal and Regina? It's easier to take two if you partial shift and hold them like this," he said.

Umm. No. Hades no. I couldn't.

Something terrifying crossed his gaze and I frowned. There was something he wasn't telling me.

'I can't fully shift. Not enough magic,' he said, and fear flooded my entire system.

Already? With each shift he was losing his power, which meant the people of Embergate were in grave danger.

I nodded, then with one jump he leapt into the air, away from the cart. Nox and Falcon hung from his arms as he flew them over the fort.

What. The. Hades?

"I don't think I can do that," I mumbled to Regina.

She looked behind me, at what I knew was the approaching gate and probably an army of more men. "You have to," was all she said, and then she and Cal reached out and grasped one of my arms each.

My leathers were hanging snugly off my waist, my breasts covered by my small bralette, and I decided that was enough clothing to remove if the goal was just to erupt wings from my back.

Pulling forth the fire within me, I pushed it into my transformation and felt a pop of pain as the wings burst from my back.

"Now!" Regina yelled and the cart jerked to a stop. I jumped into the air, flapping my wings. We went airborne, and for a few seconds I actually thought this would be easy. Then the weight of two people dragged me downward.

"Flap them harder!" Regina yelled as she held on to my left arm with two hands, and Cal held on to my right.

My wings buckled under the strain as I flapped them like a madwoman, gaining a few feet. The army was under us now, aiming up at us with arrows.

We're all dead!

I couldn't get us high enough, I was too slow, I—

An arrow whizzed right past my face and I screamed.

Regina let go of me with one of her hands, aiming at the approaching men with bows.

"No!" she yelled, an unholy look of ferocity coming across her face. Raising her hand, a stream of beautiful deadly orange fire burst from her palm and saturated the men below.

Screams filled the night, then the *thwip* of arrows cut into the sky. Pain suddenly laced into my right arm and I cried out, losing my grip on Cal for a half second. He slipped down but scrambled to hold on at the last second. I twisted to look at the source of my pain to find an arrow lodged in my right shoulder. Blood trickled down my arm and onto Cal's hands. I flapped my wings madly but we were still barely fifteen feet off the ground.

My shoulder burned like Hades but I kept going,

ignoring the numbness in my fingers. I just needed to get over the wall. It was twice as high as I was flying so I pumped my wings with everything I had.

But it was too difficult. We lost altitude, falling a few feet, and I started to whimper.

'Help me. I can't get over the wall,' I called to Drae as panic flooded my system. I was going to drop Cal any second.

"I'm trying!" I said and then looked down into Cal's and Regina's panicked expressions.

Regina looked over at Cal then, watching him slip down my arm, and then glanced up at me. "Get the king home and have an heir. Save our people, Arwen. That's an order!"

Have an heir? Why was she talking about that at a time like th—?

"NO!" The blood-curdling scream ripped from my throat as she let go of my left hand and dropped down into the fray. Cal frantically reached over and grabbed my other arm, shifting his weight to relieve my injured shoulder.

I peered down in shock as Regina pulled out her blade and then spit a stream of fire, trying to fight her way through the twenty men attacking her.

No! Not like this. It couldn't end like this.

"Regina!" A stone sank in my gut as I immediately

started to lower myself and help my beloved commander, but before I could do anything she was gored by half a dozen arrows in seconds. As if that weren't enough, a Nightfall soldier walked up and took her head clean off. Unbridled rage and wild grief filled me with equal measure, one not making enough room for the other as they smashed about within my body.

Cal squeezed my arm. "No! It will all be in vain. Get us over that wall. The king hasn't come back to help, which means he's hurt."

Cal's urging shook me from my grief. The king was hurt? Why hadn't he come back to help us, or responded to me?

I watched Regina fall forward, and my entire body flinched and went numb. It was all I needed to see to know that if I didn't get us out of here right now, we were both dead. I flapped my wings wildly, holding Cal mostly with my good arm, and soared up and over the fence now that my load was lighter. I made for the outcrop of trees that held our saddles, and hoped the king was there as well.

Regina... my idol, my mentor, the leader of the King's Drayken...

Dead.

I couldn't process it, it didn't feel real. I prayed that

I would wake up any moment and find out that Joslyn's and Regina's death were some sick nightmare.

The moment we got to the trees, I knew something was wrong. Drae was on his hands and knees, heaving up the contents of his dinner.

I landed awkwardly, tripping over my dangling feet but relieved to finally let go of Cal's weight on my injured arm.

"What's wro—?" Nausea washed over me as a cold sweat broke out over my body.

Drae stood, and I noticed that he too had been hit by an arrow. Grazed was more like it. His arm had a slight line of blood on the side.

"Regina's... dead," I said, blinking rapidly as everything blurred.

What is happening? Was losing Regina and Joslyn in the same night too much grief for my heart to bare? I felt like I was dying.

The king stomped forward, grasped the tip of the arrow in my shoulder, and yanked. I tried to scream but he covered my mouth so that I merely wailed into his salty fingers.

"Arrows are poisoned," he breathed, eyes wide as he looked over me. "Did we bring another antidote?" he called to Nox.

Nox stepped forward. "No, sir, only the one you just took."

The wild panic that consumed his face made my knees go weak.

"I'm going to die," I whimpered.

Maybe that was best. Maybe tonight would be known as the Night of Sorrows. The night when the king's betrothed, backup, and commander were all taken from him. I didn't care anymore, I just wanted to be out of pain.

"No!" He shook my shoulders and then glanced up at Cal. "Can you and the others make it back to Embergate on foot?"

Cal nodded.

"My lord, she will not survive the flight home. Dr. Elsie is too far," Falcon said.

Drae dipped his head. "I know. But we're only a few miles away from the Archmere border."

Cal's eyes widened. "You're going to the elves?"

Drae sighed. "I have no choice."

A horrible cramping seized my stomach then and I fell backwards. Drae reached out to catch me.

"Just let me go. I want to be with Joslyn and Regina," I whimpered.

He pulled me to his chest and muttered in my ear, "I can't. I *need* you."

I need you. It was something I'd wanted him to say for so long, and yet... somehow I didn't think he meant it in the way I wanted.

He needed my *womb*. Not me.

Everything got hazy then and life began to pass by in snippets.

Flying.

Drae running into an elven couples' humble home with me in his arms as he screamed in panic.

The elven woman of the household scanning me with her healing wand.

Her shaking her head to Drae that I would not make it.

More flying.

It all finally ended with an ominous-looking male towering over me. He had bright white hair and a thin silver crown on his head. I was lying on some type of crystal bed. Hard, and yet... it was not uncomfortable. It seemed to be carved out of a giant rose quartz with indentations that fit my body like a glove.

"This matter does not concern me," the male said as he stared down at me.

I rolled on my side and moaned as the cramping in my muscles became so painful I wanted to die. My heartbeat felt like it was in my ears.

"Raife," Drae growled. "She is important to me. I

know you can save her. If you do... I'll give you what-ever you want. Coal, boats, jade. Name your price!"

Raife? Raife Lightstone. The elven king? Rumor had it that he lost his entire family in one night at the hand of the Nightfall queen. His parents and seven siblings. Now he was a broken man hadesbent on revenge.

"My price?" King Raife cocked his head to the side. "Brother, my price has always been the same, and yet you deny me at every turn. You know what I want, what I require."

I moaned, a burning sensation rising up in my throat. Drae reached up and yanked on the sides of his face. "Fine, I'll help you kill the Nightfall queen if you save Arwen, but you have to get Lucien and Axil to agree to help us. She's too powerful unless we unite."

Lucien Thorne the fae king and Axil Moon the wolf king? Did Drae just agree to take down the Night-fall kingdom to save my life?

Raife reached up and rubbed his chin as if deep in thought, and Drae rushed forward. "Save her, dammit!"

The elven king rolled his eyes. "Alright, we have a deal. It may take time for me to get the other kings on board, but you *will* hold up to your promise."

I grabbed my throat, no longer able to breathe. I gasped for air.

Drae crossed a fist over his chest. "I swear it, Raife! I will help you avenge your family. Just save her!"

Raife kneeled, looming over me, bringing with him the scent of lilies. I hated lilies. They were *too* fragrant and always made me sneeze. Leaning forward, the elven king placed his nose an inch from my injured shoulder and inhaled.

"Death wood sap," he stated.

Drae rushed to the other side of me. "Can you reverse it?"

Raife looked up at Drae and I wondered how these two knew each other. Raife had called him *brother*.

"Is she the one you have chosen to have your heir?" Raife asked.

I steeled myself for his answer.

Backup.

Drae stared into my eyes, and then nodded. "If she will have me."

My heart beat wildly in my chest; blackness danced at the edges of my vision. If I were going to die, that was a pretty sweet thing to hear before I went.

Raife nodded. "Very well, then."

He laid a hand on my injured shoulder and I gasped when his skin touched mine. A flare of purple light exploded out from his palm, momentarily blinding me. Then the blackness around my vision receded and my throat stopped burning. I could finally breathe. I sucked in huge lungfuls of air. Then one by one my muscles stopped cramping and my nausea fled.

I looked up in shock at the elven king and he peered back at me with a cold and unforgiving gaze. He winced, and I wondered if healing me was causing him pain somehow. Releasing his hand from my shoulder, he held it to his chest as if it were injured.

I sat up, suddenly feeling better. "Thank you," I breathed.

He ignored me, glancing up at Drae. "Be gone by morning, I cannot have my council knowing I helped you until I get them on board with taking out Zaphira."

Drae dipped his head, and then gave King Raife a little smile. "Are they still pestering you to get married?"

Raife groaned, shaking out his fingers as if trying to expel whatever healing the poison had done to him. "I must take a wife by winter or they say they will overthrow me."

Drae smiled again, nodding, and then stepped forward, pulling the elven king into a hug. "Thank you, brother."

Raife didn't hug him back. He froze as if he had

never hugged anyone in his entire life, but Drae didn't seem to care. The dragon king pulled back, squeezed Raife's shoulders, and then turned away and headed for me.

Raife walked to the door on the far wall, and for the first time I took in the room around me: white stone floors, light purple wallpaper with flecks of gold. It was tranquil, healing.

"Drae?" Raife called from the open doorway.

Drae turned to look at the elven king.

"I *will* come for you, and we will end Queen Zaphira's reign." It was a command and a promise.

"You have my word," Drae said, and then Raife left the room and closed the door.

My tongue felt like it was stuck to the roof of my mouth. Almost dying two times in one day was too much of a shock to my system.

"Tell me you're okay." Drae kneeled before me, placing his hands on my waist and staring deeply into my eyes.

I frowned, feeling my lip quiver as tears lined my eyes. "I..." A whimper left my throat. "Joslyn... Regina," I said.

He sighed, looking down at the cold white tile. "We've let the queen go on for far too long. She has to be stopped."

"With her flight gadgets and fire throwers, I don't see how. Even with the elves. Did you see the horseless carts?"

He nodded. "Raife's parents wanted to curb her technology, knowing her plans to one day wipe out the magical races. My father denied their request for help."

I gasped. "And they tried and she killed them?"

He dipped his head. "Raife's parents blew up one of her machine factories, and in turn the queen killed Raife's entire family, leaving him alive as a mercy."

Leaving him alive after killing his entire family was a mercy?

"Why didn't you help him get revenge after she did that? It sounds like you two were close friends."

Shame colored his cheeks. "I was a young prince. My father was afraid of the Nightfall queen and counseled against helping Raife."

I nodded. "But winters later, when you became king, why did you still deny him?"

Drae looked pained at my question. "Because I'd just lost my own father, was getting married, and trying to have an heir. I didn't know the first thing about invading a territory and starting a war. To be honest, the Nightfall queen scared me. What she did to the Lightstone family frightened me."

It killed me to hear him sound so weak and vulnerable. "Does Raife know? That without an heir your magic is dead?"

He shook his head.

I sighed. I might be the backup but I was all he had, and I wasn't going to leave him when he needed me.

"Fine, you can have my royal womb," I quipped.

He stilled, going completely stiff. "Don't joke like that. I want you with or without an heir."

Now it was my turn to go completely still. "Drae, I know that you told the entire Royal Guard to stay away from me because I was your backup."

He growled. "Who told you that?"

"Cal... when I kissed him," I admitted.

His eyes flew wide. "You kissed Calston!"

"I was trying to get over you!" I punched him lightly in the chest. "But he wouldn't have me. Said he couldn't."

He leaned closer to me and looked me right in the eyes. "I ordered the other men to stay away from you because the thought of you being with another man drove me insane."

"Oh." I sucked in a breath and he reached out, tracing his finger over my bottom lip. Shivers ran down my entire body and my eyes fluttered. "Ever since Amelia died, I've felt like I was drowning. Then you walked into my life... and now for the first time I feel like I can breathe."

I gasped at the declaration. It was the nicest thing anyone had ever said to me.

"You've *never* been my backup, Arwen. You were always my first choice, ever since I saw you walking into town with that giant cougarin draped over your shoulders. I was fascinated with the beautiful and strong female hunter."

Shock ran through me. *He watched me bring my kill in?*

He stepped closer. "I peeked into the kissing tent and saw you walking towards some other guy, your lips pursed and ready. Without thinking, I jumped in front of him and took what I wanted."

I knew it was him! And the realization that he'd knowingly kissed me because he'd liked me even then, it made every brick I'd stacked around my heart crumble.

"Marry me, Arwen. Not because I need an heir but because somehow I've fallen in love with you and now I'm not sure that I can live without you."

I sucked in a breath, and in response I reached out and grasped the back of his neck, pulling his lips to mine. The second his tongue entered my mouth, there was almost a painful release within my chest. Sometimes it ached to love someone, and that was true with Drae.

He pulled back, looking down at me with uncertainty. "Is that a yes?"

I grinned. "Yes. Does this mean you're not going to kill me like my mother feared?"

He frowned. "Don't even say such a thing." He pulled up my hand and kissed each knuckle.

"Dr. Elsie said it wasn't advisable for us to have children as there was no telling what our mixed magic would create," I told him, trying to find something wrong with our union because it seemed too good to be true.

He peered down at me skeptically, no doubt wondering *how* I knew she'd said that, but I said nothing.

"Whatever we create will be a blessing upon the *entirety* of Embergate. That, I am sure of. Now, let's get home and bury our dead. Then we will tell everyone that I have chosen you as my queen."

I slipped my hand into his, and although the guilt of promising myself to the king so soon after Joslyn died weighed on me, I took comfort in the fact that it *was* him in the kissing tent all this time. I had him first.

After we gave Joslyn and Regina a respectful burial, I wanted to have him forever.

I flew us back to the castle together a few hours later in the dark of the early morning to cover us. We weren't sure how many more shifts Drae had in him, so I didn't want him to try unless he had to. Word that Drae had killed the Nightfall queen's son would no doubt have spread and we had to be on high alert. When we reached the gates of Jade City just as the sun was rising, the guards blew the horn announcing the king was back. The people flooded into the street to get a sight of their winged king, but instead of just seeing him they saw me with him riding on my back. Gasps and looks of surprise fell upon the faces of the people as they pointed and clapped and small children ran after us.

'*They are going to love you as their queen,*' Drae said into my mind.

I didn't respond. I was suddenly worried that I might have trouble conceiving with him. Then all of these people, including Adaline, would die.

'*How do you do it?*' I asked him as I lowered us over the stables and armory.

'*Do what?*'

'*Carry the weight of your entire people's fate upon your shoulders.*'

'*One day at a time.*'

I nearly cried in relief when I saw Cal, Nox and Falcon waiting for us down below. They were covered in mud and looked to be soaking wet but they were alive. They'd gotten here fast... they must have stolen horses and rode all night. Dr. Elsie stood next to them with the king's advisor, the old man with the book from my testing ceremony.

When I landed, the king got off and I ran off to the stable to dress. By the time I came out, the king was frowning. Nox, Falcon, and Cal were gone, and Drae was peering down at a small leather-bound tome.

I ran up behind him and brushed an affectionate hand over his arm and he stiffened, causing me to recoil.

Dr. Elsie stared at me with a deep sympathy that scared me, the sort of sympathy you gave before you told someone they had just lost a beloved.

I grasped my chest. "Are my mother and sister okay?"

"They're fine," Drae said, letting the book fall to his waist.

"King Valdren was just telling us of your plans to marry..." Dr. Elsie said, peering at the elderly advisor. I couldn't be sure but I thought it was he who had advised Drae to just kill me. Dr. Elsie went on: "I knew that you would be the next best option in terms of magic, so I did some research after you left."

I hated that she was constantly evaluating the fitness of my magical womb. "And...?" I asked.

"I'll speak to her alone," Drae suddenly said, and Dr. Elsie stiffened, still staring at the advisor, who looked like he was barely alive. Seriously, how old was that dude?

They scurried away and Drae turned to face me.

"Just tell me," I begged him. "I've lost Joslyn and

Regina. Just... tell me. I don't have the emotional capacity for games."

He nodded.

"There is an old book that catalogues royal births. This one was hidden due to its nature... it discusses a royal birth between Eclipse clan and Dark Night clan a thousand winters ago."

A thousand winters ago! Maybe our clans were friends back then, I didn't know.

My hands started shaking, my eyes flicking over Drae's shoulder as Elsie greeted three familiar faces in the distance.

That red-haired girl from Jade City? The blonde with the bad breath. These were girls he was courting before he chose Joslyn.

"Why are the girls back?" I asked.

Drae sighed. "After seeing this, she thought it prudent to call them. Kendal is on her way as well." He winced.

Kendal! My heart nearly seized in my chest.

What the Hades was he talking about? I reached out and ripped the book from his hands, looking down at the open page, and gasped.

The first line was in bold. **Baby severely deformed, lived only hours.**

Then I read the next line.

Hypothesis: Mother's Eclipse clan magic consumed the Dark Night clan magic, killing the child.

I didn't even know I was crying until the tears fell onto the page and wet the words.

"I can't lose another child." Drae's voice was broken.

I nodded, folded the book, and handed it back to him.

He grasped the edges of my face and forced me to look at him. "But I still want *you*."

I glanced over at the other girls. They were all talking to Annabeth and Dr. Elsie, waiting on the king no doubt.

"If I cannot give you a child, then you should not pick me," I told him truthfully. "The future of all of Embergate depends on that."

He frowned, peering over his shoulder to stare at the girls and then back at me. "What if I still married you... but I lay with them?"

I gasped.

"Purely to have a child—once pregnant I would stop. The magic of my people only needs me to have an heir. It doesn't care if that child is a bastard or not."

"You're asking me to marry you knowing you will have mistresses?" I was so hurt I couldn't even think straight.

He shook his head. "I'm asking you to spend the rest of your life with me, allowing me to bed those women once or twice in order to save thousands of lives."

I frowned. "Bed *all* of them?"

Not Kendal. *Please* not Kendal.

He swallowed hard. "Dr. Elsie thinks it will give me the best chance at success."

I chewed the inside of my lip to keep from crying as bile rose in my throat. "What you're asking feels impossible... but I'll think about it. I'd like to be alone now." I ripped my face out of his hands and then took off running through the practice fields.

"Arwen!" he yelled, but didn't come after me.

Bed three women while married to me? And not just once. It took months to get pregnant, and then if the baby died he would continue until he had a living heir.

It was hard to believe that just hours ago he was confessing his love to me and saying he wanted me to be his queen, and now he wanted to sleep with my friends? I couldn't process it.

But part of my mind thought back to my mother and what she told me about my father's seed. Was this any different than what my father had allowed to get Adaline?

Not really.

My feet pounded the grass as I cut through a lavender farm, my chest heaving with grief. I mourned the loss of three people. Joslyn. Regina. And now Drae.

The pureness that a marriage between us might have held would be defiled with three mistresses. Would he bed them and then sneak in to sleep by my side? Would he fall in love with one of them in the process?

If Drae and I were at risk of having a child who wouldn't even live more than a few hours, it meant that he'd never bed me! I'd die with my purity while my husband slept with half the realm.

No. *I can't.*

A sob ripped from my throat, startling me. I hadn't realized how much I'd allowed myself to envision a life with him. How much I'd grown to care for him and see myself by his side. I didn't know where I was going until I saw the small outcrop of weeping willows up ahead.

A resigned sigh escaped me as I ran to the comfort and devastation that those trees held. It was as if this small piece of land was a place you could fill with your sadness. Drae and Amelia filled it with the loss of their children. Then Drae filled it with the loss of her and another child. Now I would fill it with the loss of a future I would never have but was promised to me for a mere few hours. That's all it took to break someone, a few hours of hope. When ripped away it left a gaping hole that felt impossible to fill.

I knelt before Queen Amelia's grave, unsure why I'd come here, why I was standing before her resting place of all people.

Maybe because she would understand—perhaps the only person who could. They might have had an arranged marriage at first, but they had grown to love each other. She would understand my sorrow at losing the chance to be properly loved by him.

I looked out at the other small gravestones and my heart grew heavy. What had started as a simple and joyous task, having a family, had ended in horrifying loss. No parent should have an entire graveyard of their young.

None. *Not ever*.

I realized then that asking Drae to remain faithful to me would end just like this. In a field riddled with children who lived only moments. Numbness spread throughout my body as a heavy depression settled over me.

I couldn't give him what he needed, what our

people needed, and if Kendal or one of the others could... then I needed not to be selfish.

A twig snapped behind me and I spun, standing and putting my arms out to fight.

Upon seeing Drae, I relaxed and wiped at my eyes.

He looked stricken. "I should have never asked that of you. I don't know what I was thinking. I... Dr. Elsie gave me the information and I was still processing. Arwen, I love you like I've never loved another before, and—"

"It's okay." I stepped closer to him, taking his hands in mine.

I glanced over my shoulder at the gravestones. "I know what you've been through. I would never knowingly put you through that again."

He froze.

"Are you denying my hand in marriage?" His voice broke.

I shook my head, reaching out to tuck a strand of hair behind his ear. "I am not. I am simply agreeing that you should try any means possible to have an heir and save our people."

His face relaxed and his lips curled into a smile. "*Our* people."

I shrugged. "I am about to be queen after all."

Stepping closer, he stroked my cheek. "You've

always been a queen. I should have never tried to downgrade that title by putting you in my guard."

"I like being in your Royal Guard, my lord," I said formally, and he smiled.

"A king whose wife is in his army? This may be a first," he agreed.

I leaned forward and brushed my lips across his cheek. "I will admit I am disappointed that our wedding night won't be complete."

I pulled back to look up at his stormy eyes. Reaching out, he slid a hand up my thigh, causing ripples of heat to bloom between my legs. "Do not say such insane things. Our wedding night will be *more* than complete."

I frowned. "But... if we are to avoid having a child—"

He leaned forward and trailed his tongue along my collarbone, causing my legs to go weak. "There are ways to avoid pregnancy, my love."

My love. I wanted to hear him say that at least a million more times.

I threaded my fingers through his hair. "I see no reason to delay the marriage. As soon as my mother and sister can get here, we should wed."

His laughter rang throughout the space, chasing

away and breaking up some of the grief here. "Eager. I like that."

Pulling back, he nodded. "We will wed in three days. I'll send for your mother immediately."

Holy Hades. I'd just agreed to marry the king... and let him have children with someone else.

18

The funeral for Regina and Joslyn was beautiful. Regina was laid to rest, without an actual body to bury, in the Royal Guard cemetery in the north side of town, and Joslyn was buried next to the king's private family mausoleum. It was a great honor and the entirety of Jade City shut down in mourning. Drae had set Joslyn's parents up with monthly payments for the rest of their lives as they were from the poorest part of Grim Hollow and he knew they would be counting on it. Word had gotten around town that I was the Lost Royal from the stories and that I'd tried to save Joslyn's life that night. The people seemed to love me, smiling and waving happily as I passed. They knew nothing of my magic being able to suck the life from their king, and nothing of the fact that the king needed to make an heir or they would all die.

Narine told me that she had taken the liberty of spreading a rumor that the king had chosen me initially but his advisors forced him to pick Joslyn and that's why he was marrying me so quickly, that he'd loved me all along. The city loved a good bit of gossip, and they wanted their king to be happy, for which I was grateful. I would hate for there to be a rumor he'd cheated on Joslyn with me or something awful like that.

The Nightfall queen had sent back Regina's head as a message, but no other retaliation. Drae increased border patrols and sent an entire Royal Guard escort for my mother and Adaline. Now the wedding was tonight and my mother was arriving any moment.

I had no idea what she was going to think of all this. I was marrying the man she was originally scared would hurt me. But there was one thing she'd drilled into me since I was born...

Duty.

She'd say, *"You have a duty to this family, your sister, this village, me."*

Now I would have a duty to the entire dragon-folk people, and I hoped she would understand, because I planned to tell her the truth about everything. I could live with keeping secrets from a lot of people but my mother wasn't one of them.

"She's here!" Narine said excitedly as she poked her head into my room.

I stood and allowed her to fix my wedding gown. This event, our wedding, was not one I wanted to wear trousers for, though I did ask the palace seamstress to put pockets in the gown for me.

Where is a girl to keep her daggers and things if she has no pockets?

"You look... like a dream," Narine said as she creased the lace hem of my white dress.

I smiled. "Did Annabeth give you that one hundred jade coins prize money?"

Narine grinned. "I get it tonight after the ceremony. Then I'll pay you back for the—"

"Nonsense, you keep it! I'm going to be queen. I'll have more than enough money at my disposal."

Narine shook her head. "No way—"

"Keep it for your own wedding." I winked and she

blushed. I'd seen her flirting with Cal lately. "And is your sister's wedding planning going okay?" I asked.

Narine waved me off. "Yes, thanks to you. Now go see your mother and sister!"

I was stalling. To be honest, I was nervous as Hades to tell my mother I had fallen in love with the king—that I was going to marry him but could never have children with him, that instead I would be allowing him to have children with his mistresses...

What if she refused to stand by my side at the wedding? What if she left town and never spoke to me again?

With a shuddering breath, I nodded to Narine. "Please fetch her and my sister and bring them to the living room."

Narine slipped out of my bedroom and I followed her, pacing the living room and waiting. This was the last time I would be in this apartment. Tonight, I would sleep beside Drae and share a bed with him for the rest of my life.

Holy Hades, I'm going to be sick.

Was it normal to feel like you were going to vomit every few seconds on your own wedding day?

The front door opened and my mother and sister walked in with Narine in tow. They each held a small travel pack and looked at me with wide eyes as they entered. They were expected last night but there had been a sandstorm, and delays from others coming from all over the realm.

"Holy Hades, you look like a queen!" Adaline rushed over to me. "Does this make me a princess?"

She opened her arms to hug me and my mom yelled at her. "Don't touch her dress, you'll stain it."

I pulled my sister in for a bone-crushing hug, not caring about the dress. "I don't think you can be a princess but you will be a highborn lady."

Adaline pulled back to peer at me with wide eyes. "Lady Adaline?"

I nodded and she grinned.

"This is so cool."

My mother hadn't moved. There were tears in her eyes, which I didn't know how to interpret.

"Lady Adaline, would you like some chocolate cake?" Narine offered upon seeing the awkward moment between my mother and I. "I can show you the main palace kitchens and the library."

Adaline glanced to my mother, who nodded, and then she left with Narine.

I looked up at my mom then, and a single tear spilled over her cheek.

"I... I'm not sure what they told you," I fumbled.

"And I'm sorry you have to find out I'm getting married like this. It's just that—"

"You look beautiful." She stepped closer to me, reaching out to grasp my hands. "King Valdren greeted me a few hours ago as our transport party arrived outside the city, and told me his intentions with you."

He did?

"His intentions with me?" Now I wanted to know what he'd said.

"He told me that he knew about your lineage and that he would never hurt a hair on your head. That he loved you and wanted to take care of you. To have a family with you." She was smiling and I realized then that her tears were happy tears.

A family... of course he wouldn't tell my mother about our arrangement. He couldn't have a healthy family with me, that was the problem.

"Mom, sit down," I said, and her lips pulled into a frown.

She joined me on the couch and I sat next to her, careful not to mess up my dress. I loved Drae, but I was still saddened with our arrangement, and needed to unload my problems on someone else. I needed my mother's wisdom.

"Drae needs an heir or all of the dragon-folk will die."

My mother gasped, her hand going to her mouth. "Adaline."

I nodded. "His people are linked to him through a special magic that gets stronger when you reproduce but dies out if you do not by a certain age. The line must continue to carry on, no matter what."

My mom dipped her head. "I understand. Now the quick engagement and wedding makes sense. You do what you have to in order to save the people, Arwen."

My heart pinched. "That's the thing, Mom... Drae is a dragon from the Dark Night Dragon clan, I am a full-blooded dragon from the Eclipse clan."

She stilled, as if sensing this was going somewhere she wouldn't like.

"And we recently found out that my magic and his magic don't—" My throat tightened and I suddenly couldn't speak; tears filled my vision.

"Oh, honey, what is it?"

My mother was a midwife; she'd seen the worst of the worst when it came to child-bearing.

"A midwife journal was found of a royal couple like us, one Dark Night clan royal, one Eclipse clan royal. They had a child together, but... it was born severely deformed, with organs outside of its body, and only lived hours."

My mother folded in on herself then. The hopes

she might have had to have a grandchild to help raise were crushed in that moment. I could see the light die in her eyes.

"Why is he marrying you, then?" My mother looked up at me, surprised.

That simple question brought tears to my eyes, and was a true testament of Drae's love for me. "Because he loves me."

My mom nodded.

"Mom, remember when you told me that dad let you lie with another man to get Adaline?" I asked her.

Understanding dawned on my mother's face and she inclined her head, reaching out to grasp my hand. "You do what you have to do, Arwen. You're going to be a queen. You have a duty to the people of Embergate."

Duty, there it was. I knew she would say it. I wanted to do right by my sister and everyone else, but it didn't make it any easier.

I nodded. "But this is *three* women, to give him the best possible chance."

My mother winced at that but then rubbed my hand. "It will be a winter, maybe two, of wondering when he goes to them, and then he will have his heirs and you will have him forever."

"But... lying with them and then lying with me..."
A tear slipped down my cheek.

My mom wiped under my eyes. "If your father had denied me, Adaline would not exist."

It was as if she'd taken my heart and squeezed it. As much as my little sister annoyed me at times, I couldn't imagine a world where Adaline didn't exist. She was right—I knew she was right—but I still felt unsettled by the whole thing. "Thanks, Mom."

A winter or two until a healthy heir was born. I could do that. I was young and it wasn't that long.

After my mother left, I couldn't shake the feeling that I was walking into a marriage that might devastate me. I needed to see Drae and lay down some ground rules for our new arrangement. After asking Narine to settle my mother and Adaline into their guest apartment next door, I had her notify Drae that I wanted to see him. Then I paced the floor in my apartment and wrung my hands together as anxiety built up inside of me.

The door suddenly flew open and I jumped. Drae was there, wearing his black dragon scale leather printed royal armor and looking as handsome as ever. I didn't care that he was seeing me in my dress. I needed to say this to him.

"Tell me you aren't canceling the wedding." He grabbed his chest as if a physical ache had taken up residence there.

I smiled and shook my head. "I am not."

He sagged in relief and then shut the door behind him, his eyes raking over my body and the white lacy dress I wore that was a symbol of my purity.

"Are you unwell?" he asked, reaching to take my hands in his, feeling them for warmth.

I sighed. "I do not relish the idea of sharing you with other women, so I have some rules that I would like to discuss before our union."

He visibly flinched at my abruptness but nodded.

"I do not want to know when you have bedded them. Do *not* tell me."

"Of course," he agreed.

"Have a bath before you see me. I do not want to smell them on you either."

"Yes, my love." His face fell and I could see that he hadn't really thought this through. My heart hurt to even have to say any of this.

"No Kendal," I whimpered. "She is my friend from home. Try with the other two first, and if no healthy child comes from it, then Kendal is a last resort."

He pulled me into his arms and wrapped them around me. "I don't want to do this at all. I'm not sure I even can. I only want you."

A sob died in my throat. "You have to," I managed to get out. "This is bigger than just us. You have to. We will get through it together."

The realization that I would never become a mother hit me like a ton of bricks.

"I'll never be a mom," I said suddenly and he pulled away, looking at my face in horror. So he hadn't thought of it either.

"I... I'm so sorry, Arwen." He stared down at his feet and then went stock still as if realizing something. "You *could* be a mother if you bedded someone else. We could raise the child together..."

These were not conversations I wanted to have hours before my wedding. Bed another man? Have another man's child? Both of us sneaking into other people's beds? It was not the life I wanted to sign up for.

"Calston is loyal. He would... agree to an arrangement. He'd let me raise the child," Drae said, but his voice was thick with hurt.

Raise Cal's child with Drae? Bed Cal? *No.*

My voice was small. "I could never do that. I'm not capable of such a thing."

He looked relieved but also saddened. Without knowing what to do, he took me into his arms again, just holding me tightly, as if he were afraid I might run off.

We held each other for what seemed like an eternity. Finally he pulled back with narrowed eyes. "Tell me I can make you happy. That this life will make you happy. If not, I don't want to marry you and have you live in sorrow on my account."

I considered his question seriously. Would it be sad that I could never have children of my own? *Yes*. Would it kill me to know he'd bedded other women to have heirs? *Yes*.

But the alternative, living without him, him marrying Kendal or one of the others just to have an heir... it devastated me to think it.

I leaned forward and kissed his lips, pulling back to look him in the eyes. "There may be times of sorrow, I will not lie. But I do not see happiness in my life without you in it as my husband."

A devastatingly handsome grin pulled up the corners of his mouth. "I feel like I've waited my whole life to find you." He ran the pad of his thumb along my jaw.

I tilted my chin up to gaze at him. His eyes held an

adoration I wasn't sure I deserved, but I knew within my very soul that I was ready to marry this man.

"Let's wed." I leaned forward, brushing my lips across his earlobe.

A small growl emanated from his throat and I smiled, pleased with myself for eliciting such a reaction over him.

The entirety of Jade City came out for the royal wedding. The palace ballroom could not hold everyone and so they spilled out into the streets and sat upon rooftops all trying to get a glimpse of our union. Kendal attended with my mother and Adaline, but when I tried to meet her gaze she looked away in shame.

She knew. Of course she knew about the arrangement. I'm sure Dr. Elsie and Annabeth had briefed them all.

It was heartbreaking when I thought about it, so I just didn't think about it. I said yes to becoming Drae's wife, to becoming his queen, in front of the entire city. I drank wine and he drank mead. We ate chocolate cake that was the same recipe as our first date. We danced and rode around the city on horseback greeting the people. All the while, I stuffed the issues surrounding our little arrangement deep down inside of me. All of these smiling people would eventually die if Drae didn't restore the magic by giving them an heir, so any needs or thoughts I held around that were just selfish.

After a full night of revelry, my new husband brought me back to our shared room. He'd had a room of the palace never before used completely redesigned for us. No more dark wallpaper and black carpet like his old chambers. This room was full of creams and gold and felt airy and bright.

A new beginning.

I walked nervously to our shared bed, suddenly scared of the pinch of pain Kendal told me would happen when I gave up my purity.

A little pain at first for pleasure down the road, she'd informed me.

I sat at the edge of the bed and stared at Drae. As much as I wanted to make love to him, I was also nervous. He was so much more experienced than I was. He seemed to pick up on my fears as he crossed the room to kneel before me. Grasping my butt, he scooched me closer to him so that he was tucked between my legs.

"You are in charge in the bedroom, okay?" he said, and my stomach dropped out. "We can move as slow or as fast as you want."

I swallowed hard and nodded, feeling emboldened by him giving me the control. Leaning forward, I took his bottom lip into my mouth and sucked. The moan of pleasure that ripped from his throat caused me to grin. Reaching behind me, I pulled the string of the bow that held my corset together, and then shimmied out of my top half, freeing my breasts.

Drae dipped his head slowly and took my breast into his mouth, causing me to fall backwards with a moan. Heat built between us and I started to unbutton the side opening of my giant skirt. With tender hands, Drae helped undress me, pulling his own clothes off until he stood before me fully naked and fully... aroused.

I stared at his body as he lowered himself on top of me. "You're in charge," he whispered, peppering my neck with kisses. His wet tongue sent tendrils of pleasure through my body.

The heat started to pulse between my legs and I grasped one of his hands, placing it between my thighs. The second he touched me down there, rubbing small circles over my most sensitive spot, I gasped in shock. Waves of pleasure danced over me as I leaned forward and rested my lips on his shoulder, panting through the ecstasy.

He hovered over me, propped up with one arm, gazing down at me with a rakish grin. He liked my pleasure, and I wanted more.

Reaching down, I lined him up with my hips and then we came together. He slowly rocked forward and back and I hissed at the sharp stab of pain, causing him to freeze. "Are you okay?" He looked down at me with concern.

I nodded, leaning up to kiss him, and then he rocked some more. The pain was still there, but lessened with each thrust until there was just a deep throbbing which gave way to more pleasure.

Now I understood why my mother pressed upon Adaline and I to keep our purity until marriage. This was an incredibly intimate thing shared between two people. Something I couldn't imagine doing down at the tavern for one night like some of the girls did.

He started to tremble on top of me, and then

quickly pulled himself away from me, grabbing himself with his hand.

For a moment, I thought something went wrong—he'd left so abruptly—but then I realized this was the method he spoke of to make sure there was no pregnancy.

It was the most special moment of my life, giving myself fully to him, giving him something I'd saved for him alone. But my face fell when I realized that he would soon be sharing this moment with other women. That we would never have a child together.

He peered over and scanned my face, worry taking over his as he seemed to understand what I was thinking.

"It won't be like that with them. I won't kiss them, I'll barely touch them, just enough contact to get the job done."

A single tear slid down my cheek, running behind my neck and I realized that our marriage was doomed from the start. I'd never truly be okay with this arrangement. It would fester inside of me until I exploded. I learned in that moment that I was a horribly jealous woman who didn't want to share one inch of my husband. Not even to save a kingdom.

But I said nothing, because I knew if I did he would back out of the arrangement, and Adaline and everyone I loved who carried dragon magic would die.

The next morning we made love two more times, staying in bed until midday. Finally, we bathed and got dressed to have lunch in the dining hall. Drae promised to take me on a two-day trip to Grim Hollow. I'd never seen the shipping port, which was famous for its wares from beyond the realm and was full of trader stalls and markets.

We were going to have lunch and plan out the trip, but when we stepped into the dining room, Cal and Falcon burst in through the other doors just as the horns of war blew from the city gates.

Without hesitation, Drae took off running toward where Cal and Falcon stood.

They murmured something to him and Drae looked at me. "Stay here, my love!" he shouted, and they all ran down the hall, presumably for the barn to ride to war.

Like Hades I'm waiting here! Just because I was his wife didn't mean he could tell me what to do. I jogged after them, grateful I'd worn trousers and a small tunic today.

"The Nightfall queen has taken Middle Bridge. Our army is keeping her back, but barely," Cal said as they ran.

I jogged up beside the three of them, passing Annabeth on the way, who flattened herself against the wall in fear as we passed.

"The king and I will fly to lend aid," I said.

Drae stared at me and shook his head. "You must stay back and keep safe."

I growled, an almost inhuman growl which caused all three men to glance over at me in shock. "I am still a member of the Royal Guard, sworn to protect you. I will fight and you will *not* tell me what to do."

His eyes narrowed. Cal looked like he was hiding a grin.

"The queen has spoken," Falcon said. "We could use her power, sir. Especially after losing Regina."

Her name hung in the air like a tangible thing. Her loss was felt deeply in that moment. She would know what to do, she would call the shots. Drae hadn't even replaced her yet. I believed a part of him didn't want to accept she was really gone.

"A queen who fights in the Royal Army?" Drae said as we burst outside to the chaos of the entire Royal Guard suiting up for battle.

I nodded. "That's right."

He just sighed in resignation but said nothing. We stepped into the barn; the others stayed outside to give us privacy while we shifted. I no longer turned away from him, this time taking off my clothes before him while he watched me with yellow glowing eyes.

"Are you sure it's okay that you use your magic to shift?" I asked him.

He inclined his head. "I'll just attempt a partial shift of my wings. We could use two fliers."

I pulled on my magic and then was thrust forward as the shift took over my body. I was on my hands and knees as I heard Drae grunting above me, bones snapping as he completed his own shift.

A growl of frustration ripped from Drae's throat. I looked over at him in my dragon form now that my change was complete. He was shirtless, on his knees, half of a wing protruding from his back, black scales on his face and one hand turned to a claw.

My heart plummeted into my chest. *'What's wrong?'* I asked, using our mental link.

His chest heaved up as he stared at me with pure shock marring his beautiful features.

"I... I can't shift." His words slammed into me like arrows and I stumbled backwards until my tail hit the backside of the barn.

No. No... we weren't ready for this. Not now, not while we were under attack.

He seemed shocked into silence, and so I channeled my inner Regina and took charge. I looked him right in the eyes. '*Get dressed. Get my saddle, and ride on my back as a bowman.*'

He stood there wide-eyed, as if hoping something might change. He'd waited too long to have an heir. His parents only had one child before his mother died in labor with their second.

We were out of time.

"My men will wonder why I don't ride in my dragon form," he said, shame marring his deep voice.

'*Tell them your wing is injured. Or better yet, tell them not to question their king. Let's go!*' I urged him. Every second we stood here talking, the Nightfall queen got closer to taking our Middle Bridge territory.

He got moving then, changing his one hand and wing back to human and then throwing on clothes. Within moments, he had secured my saddle and sat on my back holding a bow. As I walked out to the rows and rows of men dressed for battle, my heart was with my husband, my king. The queen was retaliating for her son, and I wasn't going to let anything happen to Drae in his weakened state.

If he died, if they all died, I would be the only one

with dragon magic left... and that thought was too terrifying, so I pushed it aside.

The men looked confused for a moment at seeing Drae riding on my back, but he started to bark orders and they quickly fell into line.

"Meet us at Middle Bridge!" he yelled, and then I took flight.

He was heavy, so my initial liftoff was wobbly, but pretty quickly I was able to balance myself and control my wing speed in order to smooth out the ride.

I flew faster than I ever had before, the drums of war beating throughout the entire kingdom. Below us, warriors rode to Middle Bridge on horseback. I squinted to try and make out anything in the distance. On the horizon ahead I saw smoke wafting up from Middle Bridge.

'They're burning it!' I shouted.

Middle Bridge was our only way through the Narrow Strait and into Thorngate, where we traded with the fae. A third of the food we consumed came from trade with Thorngate. This would devastate us. Anger swirled inside of me. Metal specks glinted in the sky and I knew it wasn't birds.

'Take down the human fliers,' I told him.

'On it,' he replied and I drew closer, watching in awe as he expertly shot arrows while standing on my

back. One by one, the flying humans dropped from the sky like stones, and I focused my sights on the bridge below. The fire was small, just at the beginning of the bridge, and our warriors were trying to put it out with buckets from the river. At the end of the bridge, the entrance to the Narrow Strait, was the queen of Nightfall. I'd never seen her in person, but I could not mistake the regal woman on horseback wearing a red leather battle suit and a tall golden crown. Her arms glinted with metal from the contraptions strapped there. Her face was pulled into a grimace.

'Arwen, no! She's too powerful,' Drae said, but I was already flying at her. She was right there in front of me. One stream of fire and the world would be rid of her. She was weak, a simple human. If I didn't take her out now, she'd keep coming for me and Drae and his future children.

"Arwen!" He slapped my shoulder as if trying to steer me another way.

I built the fire up inside of me, ready to blast her with it, when her head snapped up in my direction. I'd been wrong to mistake her for a weak human, but I realized that too late. In one swift move she leapt into a standing position on her horse's back and raised her arms. One second she was pointing at me and the next a dozen metal bolts flew from the device on her forearm right for Drae and I like comets falling from the sky.

I prayed he was strapped in as I did a roll midair to avoid the metal projectiles.

'Holy crap! Are you okay?' I asked Drae as I straightened out.

'I'm fine. Don't get too close to her! That thing on her arm is shooting way farther and faster than I can with my bow.'

I nodded my dragon head, still shaken by the whole thing.

'What do we do? They can't take that bridge. We won't survive the winter without the fae crops.'

The queen looked delighted at my retreat. She dismounted her horse and walked to the other side of the bridge that wasn't yet burning. There was a glint of steel and a small flame flickered in her palm.

Stupid machine contraptions!

She was going to take the bridge.

'Burn her forest!' Drae bellowed. *'If she wants to take our bridge, we take her land too.'*

Yes!

It was brilliant.

Veering to the left, I flew outside the rocky cobble-stone path of the neutral Narrow Strait and into Night-fall territory.

An arrow flew from the trees but I dodged it, and then swooped low into the thick forest. When I was a few feet from the tree line, I released all the magic I'd been holding in a blue stream of deadly fire.

I flew low, spreading the flames across the tops of as many trees as possible, not even stopping when I reached a wooden guard tower. The tower ignited, and a man screamed, jumping out of it and towards the ground.

"Retreat!" I heard the queen bellow. "Fetch water."

I started to turn back towards the bridge as the Nightfall warriors scattered like ants. They abandoned the bridge and ran from the river to the now-burning forest. I stayed far from the queen's range of shot, but close enough that I could see her face.

She looked livid, her mouth contorted in an evil grimace, and it brought me great joy. The bridge fire was dying down as our people splashed it with water. The wood was charred black in parts but it would hold.

For now.

The Royal Guard cheered as I flew over them, circling to make sure the queen didn't try to come back and burn the bridge, or worse, enter our lands. But she was busy enough trying to contain her own fire, which had now spread to three times as many trees as I'd ignited. She'd have her hands full for weeks, maybe even months, if it spread to buildings.

I landed and let Drae talk with his men, checking on them and doing an inventory of injured warriors. After everything calmed down, he ordered them to keep a presence there and to start making plans for a bridge made of stone. Once we felt the situation was handled, he climbed back on my saddle and I flew us home.

As I landed on the ground of the palace, Dr. Elsie rushed forward and examined me for injuries. Drae dismounted, pulled off the saddle, and I shifted and changed into clothes.

"I'm fine. Check him," I told her, spinning to find Drae staring at me with concern.

"I'm fine too," he said.

I shook my head and widened my eyes. "Tell her."

Dr. Elsie frowned. "Tell me what?" She had her healing wand ready.

He sighed as Dr. Elsie looked confusedly between the both of us. Stepping forward, I lowered my voice. "His magic is..."

I couldn't speak it out loud; the thought terrified me.

"Dying. I can no longer even partial shift," Drae finished, and Dr. Elsie's face fell.

"Well, then you know what you must do. Tonight." There was an urgency to her voice.

Drae nodded in understanding and then she left us.

It was like a knife to the chest, how quickly she determined that my husband needed to bed another woman.

She'd broken one of our rules without knowing it. A rule that was supposed to keep me sane throughout all of this. I didn't want to know when.

Now I knew and I wouldn't sleep. I'd chew off every fingernail. I'd pace holes into the carpet.

Tonight.

"I don't want to." His voice was low as his arms came around me, holding me while he breathed down my neck.

The side door opened and Adaline stepped out, completely unaware of what she was walking into, and upon seeing my beloved little sister I nodded. "You must."

I wouldn't let Adaline and everyone else die on account of my jealousy.

Spinning, I kept my emotions in check as I kissed his cheek. "I'm going to have dinner with my mother and sister tonight," I informed him.

He went very still, watching me like an animal

watches its prey, trying to see through the façade I was putting on. I wanted to sob, I wanted to slap him, I wanted to make love to him.

I did none of it.

"I love you," I said, then stepped away from him and beckoned my sister.

My first duty as queen was to save my people. Only the people had no idea, and they never would.

I moved my food around my plate a lot at dinner but didn't eat. Adaline didn't seem to notice but my mother did. She frowned, looking at me as my heel bopped on the carpet nervously. We spoke of the weather, the fig trees, and every other boring thing, and after a while I bid them goodnight.

I paced the carpet of our luxurious bedroom and stared at our marital bed. Thinking of the way he bedded me last night made heat bloom between my legs, but thinking of him doing that to other women caused smoke to steam from my nostrils. I walked over to the bed, picked up a pillow, and threw it across the room in frustration. My mother had once told me it was hard to tell when a woman's good fertile days were, so she advocated daily bedding for the couple trying to conceive. The thought of Drae doing this nightly made bile rise into my throat.

Why did I tell him it was okay? I suddenly regretted giving him permission to do such a thing. I wanted to run down the halls of the palace screaming his name and then attack whichever woman was under him right now. I wasn't cut out for this, not now, not ever.

Grasping a porcelain teacup, I threw it against the wall with a scream. When it shattered, splashing hundreds of broken pieces across the sofa, I felt no better.

Desperation gripped me. Then the door blew open, slamming into the wall so hard that I jumped. A yelp of surprise ripped from my throat and I spun, my gaze raking over Drae's shirtless form.

A single tear stained his cheek and he shook his head as he closed the door behind him. A tear, a head shake. What did it mean?

I was frozen in time, locked in my mind trying to analyze the situation. Was he mad? Did I do something wrong? Had the women rejected him?

When he reached me, he grasped my hips. "I can't. I won't."

Four words. Four small words was all it took to deepen my love for him.

"I want a baby with *you*. I want to be the father of *your* child, and I want you to be a mother," he said.

My lip quivered as tears rolled down my cheeks unencumbered. "But... if it's deformed—"

"I don't care. I will love whatever child we make together for however long we have with him."

My heart nearly grew wings in that moment and I feared it would fly out of my chest. A king so consumed with bloodline didn't care if he had a child with a defect? It was unheard of. The Nightfall queen once killed one of her sons for having a stutter.

"Him?" I quirked an eyebrow.

He grinned. "Or her."

His hands moved from my waist to my stomach, and I thought about the gravity of the situation. Wasn't having a child you knew would be born in discomfort wrong? "It's not right to put a child through pain for our selfishness," I said.

"One journal entry doesn't mean every child between that couple was born with an ailment. These things happen. It could have been just the first baby but not the others. They could have had five more healthy children between them." It was as if the dark cloud that had been following me around all day had parted in the sky.

He was right. My mother told me these things did

327

happen. Cruel twists of fate with no cause. I wished this couple were still alive today to ask them.

A child having a condition didn't make them any less, and I would love whatever little one we created. It would be half me and half Drae.

"If the child lives for only a moment, does it still strengthen your magic?" I asked.

He nodded. "The moment you get pregnant, my magic will strengthen a bit, then fully at the birth."

I was suddenly overcome with adoration for this man. He chose me, he chose us, in all our imperfections, and that was pretty perfect to me.

Nine moons later.

"She's in pain. Do something!" Drae barked to Dr. Elsie.

The dragon-elf healer rolled her eyes at the king. "She's in labor! Pain is expected."

My mother stood from my side and walked over to Drae, who was pacing the carpet. He stopped, looking down at her with frantic, wild eyes. He'd been to every one of Amelia's labors, lost four children, and a wife last time—this was very traumatic for him. I told him he didn't need to be here but he'd have none of it. He said he wouldn't leave my side.

"I know you're scared," my mother said. "But I've seen many women through childbirth and they weren't half as strong as my Arwen. She's going to be fine."

He all but fell into her arms for a hug and my throat tightened with emotion. Adaline and my mother had moved into the palace when I'd announced my pregnancy, and my mother and husband formed a special bond. She had a way of calming him; he respected her and valued her wisdom.

I grunted as another tightening took hold of my stomach. It had been a pretty easy pregnancy. No sickness like other women complain of; Drae fed me chocolate cake every night and whatever else I wanted, and gave me foot massages. But the labor was far from easy.

The elf king, Raife, had done us a kindness and engaged the queen in a small skirmish, and she'd lost interest in us... for now.

I screamed as pain took hold of my body, and both my mother and Drae rushed to my side, each one taking a hand. It felt like the area between my legs was on fire.

"It burns," I grunted, trying to push hard like my

mother taught me over the last few months of coaching sessions.

"I see the head!" my mother said, getting into position between my legs.

Dr. Elsie grasped a blanket and a basin of sterile water and rushed beside my mother. We agreed that my mother would tend to me, and Dr. Elsie, who had more experience, would tend to the child and its... complications. Whatever they might be.

Drae's head leaned against my shoulder. He spoke barely above a whisper. "I've loved you more than anything in this world," he breathed into my ear.

I realized then that he was preparing for me to die, and it shocked and saddened me.

"Tell me that again when I'm *actually* on my deathbed."

Pressure built, and I growled as pain like I'd never felt before sliced between my legs, like a butcher knife cutting my most sensitive parts.

The pressure was so intense I almost passed out. Then there was relief.

"A girl!" my mother said with joy, and I looked down, shocked. I braced myself for deformities, organs outside the little one's body, an unbreathing child, blue skin, but... she was perfect. A golden glow dropped from the ceiling then and covered the baby, causing the breath to catch in my throat.

Was that the magic? The dragon magic that fed to our people? The second it hit her skin, it was gone almost as if I'd imagined it.

I burst into tears, and realized that Drae's head was still down. He couldn't bring himself to look up. He was probably afraid of another stillborn. That's when our daughter let loose with a big cry and Drae's head snapped up.

I studied his face, wanting to commit this moment to memory forever—the moment he had a healthy child.

"Elsie, check her heart, her lungs, her..." A sob formed in his throat.

"She's fine. I just scanned her." Elsie held up her wand.

Drae sobbed, holding his hand over his mouth, no longer able to hold in the emotions. My mom stood and went to hand the baby to me, when the pressure built between my legs again. I grunted in pain, wild-eyed as I stared at my mom. "Something's wrong," I said, and Drae's entire body went rigid.

My mom handed the baby to Drae and he took her, holding her as if she were a delicate egg. "What's going on? Is she bleeding? That's how it happens, the woman bleeds too much," he said.

My mother shook her head. "It's probably just the afterbirth—" Her breath caught in her throat as she looked between my legs.

"Push!" she shouted, and my abdomen went rock hard. I leaned forward, not really sure what was happening, and pushed.

Fire. *Pressure*. And then *relief*.

A second cry split through the room and Drae and I stared at each other with wide eyes.

"Twin girls," my mom said with joyous laughter.

"Two?" Drae peered down at the daughter in his arms, and then the one in my mother's. She leaned on the bed and handed the second child to me. She too was covered in that golden magic that lingered for only seconds before disappearing.

She was perfect. Soft skin, blue eyes, a button nose. Twins. It was so rare, and there was no way of knowing until you got in labor. I couldn't help the laughter that bubbled out of me.

Two girls.

"Regina and Joslyn, that's what I want to name them," I said to Drae.

He nodded, and then sat on the edge of the bed

and looked down at the tiny child in his arms. "Two princesses."

I grinned. "You'll be the last dragon king for a while."

The smile grew wider on his lips. "I'm okay with that."

He lay back, snuggling into me as we held our girls between us. Sometimes life was hard and horrible things happened, but we were proof that even the darkest times could be turned into a happily-ever-after.

My mother tended to me and cleaned the girls. Drae and I just lay there staring at them in wonder. Joslyn had fuzzy blond hair like me, but Regina's hair was darker like her father's.

"I can feel the magic coursing through me. It's so strong," Drae said.

With two heirs now, I hoped so. It was a great relief. Adaline and everyone else I cared about would be okay.

There was a knock at the door, and Drae called out for them to enter.

Cal walked in, took one look at the two girls and bowed his head, smiling. "Twins? Congratulations."

"Thank you," we said in unison.

The smile fell from his lips as he peered at the king. "My lord, there is an urgent matter to discuss."

Drae frowned. Calston wouldn't intrude moments after my birth if it truly were not urgent.

"You may discuss it freely before my wife and queen," Drae said.

Cal cleared his throat. "King Raife Lightstone is in your study."

Drae jerked into a sitting position, looking down at little Regina and then to me. If Raife was here, it meant he was here to make good on Drae's promise. He was here to ask my husband to start a war.

"Go," I told him, trying to keep the shakiness from my voice. Raife wouldn't come all the way over here if it weren't serious. I owed my life to that man, and even though war brought death and hardship, I was in agreement that the Nightfall queen had to be stopped.

My mother took baby Regina from Drae and he crossed the room, taking one last look at me and smiled.

I loved that smile. I loved that all he'd done since I'd met him was smile more and more each day. I liked to think it was because of me. No matter what this war brought, we had each other and our new little family of four.

Drae

I'd wanted to marry Arwen the first time I laid eyes on her. She'd been carrying a ninety-pound cougarin through the woods, with an injury bleeding down her back. She was alone, which told me she was a confident hunter, and even covered in dirt and blood she was the most beautiful woman I'd ever seen. Leaving her moments after the birth of our children was not something I wanted to do, but Raife knew Arwen was set to deliver any day now; he'd sent a gift basket. He wouldn't just come in person to congratulate us.

Something was wrong.

Would he demand I go to war with the queen now? Moments after finally becoming a father? When Raife and I were six years old, our parents had us attend a "princes summer camp." It was a yearly four-week camp where Raife, Lucien of the fae, Axil of the wolves, and myself all bonded. Our parents thought it would keep the supernatural kingdom strong should the queen ever come after us. Then at fourteen, when Raife's parents were murdered, he sent a letter to Lucien, me, and Axil, begging us to help avenge them. We were just kids, and our parents had said it was an elven problem so we couldn't get involved. Raife stopped talking to us then, and the yearly retreats stopped.

He became king at age fourteen... I couldn't imagine.

When I finally became King at eighteen winters old, Raife came to my coronation ceremony and again asked me to help him avenge his parents. My first day as king and he wanted me to declare a *war*?

I couldn't. Not with my own issues ongoing. My father dying meant the dragon magic fully relied on me, and without an heir of my own I couldn't just charge into *war*.

That was over four winters ago. Now I had two heirs. If Raife asked me to go to war today, I would not deny him.

I opened the door to my office, ready to say yes to whatever it was he would demand of me. I would not forget he saved my beloved Arwen from certain death. I was a wise king now, with a powerful army at my disposal. There was a lot I could grant if he asked. I didn't relish the idea of taking on the Nightfall queen when I now had two newborns, but I knew Arwen would support me after Raife had saved her life.

Had he gotten Lucien and Axil to agree already? That was hard to believe considering he was dealing with his own council's insistence that he get married lest they unseat him. I'd hoped it would take several winters before he actually came to me ready to start this war. People would die on all sides, and I wasn't keen to hasten something like that, but the Nightfall queen had to be stopped. This we agreed on.

I stepped into the room and found him sitting in my chair, running his fingers over my desk.

He looked up at me and smiled. "Are congratulations in order?" His relaxed demeanor calmed me down. Maybe he really did just come here to give his well wishes. We had been sending letters back and forth, trying to rebuild a broken friendship.

I nodded. "Twin girls. Healthy."

He stood, walking out from behind my desk. "Twins? Great news!"

My gaze fell to his hand and the ornate wedding ring he now wore.

"And congratulations to you as well. I'm sorry we couldn't make the wedding, but with Arwen so heavily pregnant—"

He waved me off. "It's fine. Listen, I have intel you need to know, and I couldn't tell you about it via courier."

I could feel the frown pulling at my lips. I was tired. I had been up all night worrying about Arwen. I still couldn't believe she was alive and healthy and I now had two daughters. It didn't feel real. I wished Amelia were here to see it. She'd been my best friend; she would be so happy for me today. Amelia and I had always known our fates were tied together since birth; we'd never been given another choice. She'd once asked me that if I weren't betrothed to her, what kind of woman I'd desire. I was twelve at the time so I'd answered honestly.

My dream woman would have hair the color of moonlight, she'd want to hunt and shoot bow and arrow with me and my friends, she wouldn't fuss over dresses and fashion, and she'd eat normal portions of food, not pick at salads like a bird.

Amelia had laughed and told me that woman didn't exist. I didn't know it at the time but I'd been describing Arwen.

"Drae?" Raife peered at me with concern, pulling me from my thoughts.

I shook my head, reaching up to rub my face. "I'm sorry. I haven't slept. What is it?"

Raife ran a shaky hand through his hair. "I... don't even know where to begin."

Chills ran the length of my arms. This was worse than I thought. Raife was never at a loss for words.

"Is it the Nightfall queen?" I started.

Did she kill his new wife? He didn't look like he was in mourning. More like he was afraid. The elf king feared nothing.

He nodded, looking up at me with dread in his eyes. "She's... she has a new machine."

That woman and her machines. For someone who didn't like magic, she sure tried to replicate it with technology.

"What does it do?"

He let out a long-suffering sigh. "It strips a person of their magic, making them human. A magical castration of sorts."

"Hades," I cursed, a spine-tingling chill settling into my bones. This was it; this was how she would finally reach her goal of a human world, devoid of any magical creatures.

"My people don't survive without our dragon magic. It feeds our human self," I told him. "This would be death for us."

Raife nodded. "That's why I came to tell you as quickly as I could. We have to warn Lucien and Axil. We need to unite and ready for war."

I swallowed hard. "You want to go see Lucien? I can fly to Fallenmoore and see if I can find the reclusive wolf king."

Raife cleared his throat. "I tried that on my way here."

I spread my hands wide. "What's the problem?"

The elf king reached up and rubbed the back of his neck. "He tried to kill me."

I grinned, somehow knowing there was a story with this. "And why would he do that?"

Raife sighed. "I went through a few dark years, and I may or may not have slept with the love of his life while I was visiting Thorngate on business."

I barked out in laughter, clasping my old friend by the shoulders. "Is that why he's such a miserable fool now?"

Raife winced. "I need you to go with me to see Lucien. Then we can get him to go with us to see Axil. The wolves have grown in number. I hear them on my borders at the full moon. We need everyone. Axil always liked Lucien the best."

It was true. Lucien and Axil were thick as thieves at our yearly retreats.

"My wife just had twins," I told him, giving him a stern look.

Raife growled. "The queen tried to poison me again a few moons ago. Zaphira *must* be stopped before there are none of us left to fight her."

I frowned. After poisoning his entire family, she was still trying to kill him?

I wouldn't forget how she'd come into my own garden and killed Joslyn. Was she trying to take out all the kings? "Alright. Give me a week with my beloved new family and then I will meet you in Thorngate to talk to Lucien."

Raife clapped me on the shoulders. "I knew I could count on you."

Earning back Raife's trust was important to me, and this world would not be safe for my wife and daughters so long as Zaphira and her evil machines still lived.

It was time to protect what I loved most. No matter the cost.

The End.

Want to know what happens next with Raife Lightstone? Click here to preorder book two.

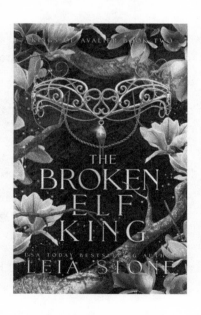

And book three...

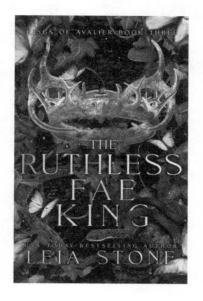

And book four =)

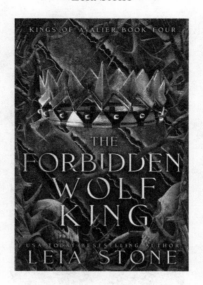

Acknowledgments

Always a big thank you to my amazing readers! I truly could not do this without you. It still amazes me that I get to be creative and do this for a living and someone actually wants to read what I write. Thank you to my Wolf Pack who is so supportive. To my editors Lee and Kate, I am a sloppy mess without you. And always to my husband and children for sharing me with my art. <3

Leia Stone is the USA Today bestselling author of multiple bestselling series including Matefinder and Wolf Girl. She's sold over two million books and her Fallen Academy series has been optioned for film. Her novels have been translated into five languages and she even dabbles in script writing. Leia writes urban fantasy and paranormal romance with sassy kick-butt heroines and irresistible love interests. She lives in Spokane, WA with her husband and two children.

facebook.com/leia.stone

instagram.com/LeiaStoneAuthor